Praise for Alex Beecroft's
Under the Hill: Dogfighters

"This brisk and engrossing sequel to *Bomber's Moon* is...a treat for readers who like their romance with a healthy dose of adventure."

~ *Publishers Weekly*

"WOW! I thought Part 1 (*Bomber's Moon*) was fantastic, and this is just as astounding—a fast-paced, edge-of-your-seat ride to the end. Superb."

~ *Reviews by Jessewave*

"In terms of style, originality, aesthetic richness, conceptual depth, and just plain FUN these books are among the best I've ever read."

~ *Violetta Vane, author of* The Druid Stone

Look for these titles by *Alex Beecroft*

Now Available:

Captain's Surrender
Shining in the Sun

Under the Hill
Bomber's Moon
Dogfighters

Under the Hill: Dogfighters

Alex Beecroft

Samhain Publishing, Ltd.
11821 Mason Montgomery Road, 4B
Cincinnati, OH 45249
www.samhainpublishing.com

Under the Hill: Dogfighters
Copyright © 2013 by Alex Beecroft
Print ISBN: 978-1-61921-055-4
Digital ISBN: 978-1-60928-725-2

Editing by Anne Scott
Cover by Lyn Taylor

This book is a work of fiction. The names, characters, places, and incidents are products of the writer's imagination or have been used fictitiously and are not to be construed as real. Any resemblance to persons, living or dead, actual events, locale or organizations is entirely coincidental.

All Rights Are Reserved. No part of this book may be used or reproduced in any manner whatsoever without written permission, except in the case of brief quotations embodied in critical articles and reviews.

First Samhain Publishing, Ltd. electronic publication: May 2012
First Samhain Publishing, Ltd. print publication: April 2013

Dedication

To all the readers who didn't throw the book at the wall after the cliffhanger in volume one.

Chapter One

With a lithe movement, Oonagh swung her leg over the dragon's ridge and slid to the ground. Here she proved taller than Flynn remembered. Seven feet tall and willowy, shiny and black as polished obsidian. She had changed herself, as casually as Flynn might change a jacket, in order to match her steed, and the only patch of colour between the two of them was the dragon's red and amber eye, fixed with reptilian curiosity on the little golden birds of Sumala's headdress.

"I must confess, I'm disappointed." Oonagh drifted close enough for Flynn to touch. She had done this to him. She had ordered his plane shot down. She had been the one. How right that she should be the colour of soot, like the inside of the Lanc's Perspex once it had been coated with burning airman.

He thought of grabbing her, putting a hand around her throat and squeezing. But despair was still reverberating in him like the aftereffects of a struck gong. He felt as though he stood at the bottom of the ocean, miles down, submerged beneath the pressure of tons and tons of grief. It was so heavy he couldn't move.

While he thought, the queen's guards fell into place around her, their long spears gleaming with viscous, almost living light. The elf guard were all sharpness, even the silver glints from their armour fell on the eye like razors.

"It cost us some pains, finding out exactly what the prophecy meant," Oonagh went on. Her bare feet did not sink into the marsh. The white flash of her chain upon chain of diamonds had a pinprick glitter. Like Sumala, she had left off other clothes, except for a black hooded cloak beneath which she was clad entirely in jewels. Unlike Sumala, her figure was warlike, tall and honed and sturdy. She noticed him looking and swept out a hand in what seemed a gesture of invitation. With the spear tips behind it, it was a command. "Walk with me."

She led the way back to the oaken causeway, through thickets of gorse that came into bud as she passed. The silver eyes she affected today gleamed with the same edge as her guardsmen's knives when she looked sidelong at Flynn's shell-shocked face. "Nor were you and your friend easy to locate. We have the promise that you will prove instrumental in saving me from a great threat..."

"As long as I am not dead." Flynn thought about suicide. Rumours that some divisions had been issued with cyanide pills for just that purpose had proved in the end only rumours, but now he thought, *If only.*

Oonagh smiled. Her skin had the texture of hot tar and the smile looked greasy as a result. "Ah, yes. As long as you were neither dead nor alive. And which would you say you were?"

A new horror joined the sick realisation in his stomach and made the tic above his eye start up, maddening as the drip drip drip of water torture. Alive, he'd said, confidently enough to Liadain, but that was before he'd seen his harness rot into the ground in seconds.

Neither alive nor dead? Huh, yes. How remarkably appropriate. He felt in his pocket for the final stub of his last cigarette, only to find he had already used his last match. So, it seemed destiny did own the fates of men after all. Free will was only so much hogwash and wishful thinking, and he was doomed, ever since he made that first bargain with the hag, to end up somehow supporting the elvish equivalent of Hitler.

Oonagh's dragon performed a strange leaping hop in an attempt to keep up. Unlike the queen herself, the creature had sunk deeply into the mud, had to use all its wing power to pull itself out with a pop and a whiff of marsh gas. It came down before them on the firmer bank of the river, swam out into the stream to get clean. Sumala, surrounded by guards, ran and squatted on the bank, calling to it. It leaned its chin on the reeds in front of her, and he could hear them whispering to each other, she in a barely audible murmur, it in a hiss like iron quenched in a bucket.

"What do you want of me?" Flynn asked Oonagh. He was surprised at Sumala's seeming carefree attitude. A moment ago she'd seemed to understand that something dreadful had happened. Now she was off, making new friends.

A lurch of guilt caught the thought up as concern for her fought a weary battle with his own selfish misery. Why was he thinking badly of the girl when she had just given up her own escape for his sake? Yet why had she been so ready to do so?

He wondered if Liadain was right. Was Sumala's real purpose to stick with him, to control him? If that was the case, then of course she would have turned down the chance of being sealed in a different world from him. Was she being noble, a good friend? Or had she just proved herself a spy?

Oonagh put a firm hand on his shoulder, breaking these uncomfortable thoughts. "I want you to do what you have been brought here to do."

He shrugged it off, there was a tickly charge to the touch, and he didn't want her reassurance. "I won't help you invade other countries, enslave their inhabitants and plunder their resources. I don't care what I'm destined to do. I won't do that."

Accepting the rebuff, Oonagh climbed up to the lip of the riverbank. The fog was breaking up and streaming away, and it seemed for a moment as if she were the lightning in the centre of the cloud. Then the sun broke through, and she dazzled so bright he couldn't look. "My poor child," she said. "I *cannot* invade anyone's country, and no one can invade mine. No one comes in or out of this realm without the permission of one of its queens. That is how it is for the queens and kings of all worlds. Only your own is as leaky as a sieve. That is because the human world has killed its king and half destroyed itself in the process. I think you have been speaking to someone who has told you lies about me."

She had a plausible voice. He felt compelled to believe her, and even as he noticed and resented the compulsion, Sumala said, "That's true. And that's why you had to kidnap me, because you thought that if you had me as a hostage my father would have to agree to open his realm to let me back. Then you could take your warships into his country and have it for yourself. Well, I won't let you, and neither will he."

"Someone has been saying remarkable things to you both." The queen beckoned, and her dragon set its great claws in the bank and heaved itself like a crocodile onto the land.

"Someone should be eaten," it said, in a voice like wind through gravel. "A moment's snack and it's done." It laid its head down in front of Flynn, and its muzzle alone came up to his thigh. With its jaw on the ground, it and he regarded one another eye to eye.

There was a whole universe of fire in its gaze, welcoming him into cave upon cave of gold and amber, maze upon maze of riddles. He saw himself briefly as it must see him, in monotone, surrounded by a lapping cloud of something. It looked like smoke. No, it didn't *look* like anything—it *tasted*, he tasted of weariness and confusion and despair.

He was leaving a vapour trail of homesickness behind him. It tasted the washed-out blue of a woodpigeon's breast and smelled like frankincense. Flynn shook his head, stepped back, and Sumala put herself between the mocking yellow gaze and him. "Leave him alone!"

The rumble of dragon laughter was like stones falling. Its face did not change shape, but it raised its wings as a dog might raise alerted ears. "He is not above a mouthful, but I would have trouble getting the taste out of my mouth afterwards. You, on the other hand, covered in gold..."

It slid out a long, bright blue tongue and lashed the air around her. "I could crunch the bones, melt the gold and spit it out to add to my hoard. You are a toothsome morsel."

Hands on hips, Sumala stared it down, and at last the avalanche of laughter came again. Flynn thought, for one mad moment, that it winked at him, the glow in one eye fading, flicking back on.

"Up you come then," it finished with ghastly cheer, jerking its chin to gesture them up. At the same time, one of the guards jabbed Flynn in the back with his spear, and the energy in it gave him an acid zing, as if his blood had turned to lemon juice.

He staggered but managed to stay on his feet, propping himself on the dragon's neck ridges. A murmur went through the onlooking warriors, and the one who had struck him stepped back, looking frightened.

As he pushed himself upright, the dragon's neck surprisingly warm beneath his palm, the scales smooth but not slimy, it occurred to him that they had expected him to fall over, unconscious, and he remembered, belatedly, how much stronger he was than they.

Could that help him now? Could he turn, unexpectedly, fight them all and... And what? Certainly not go home. So what else was there to do? He looked speculatively at Oonagh, who was leaning on her own spear, quite calmly, waiting for him to do as he was told.

The skipper would have fought her just for that. Just because he didn't like to be told what to do. But Flynn would never see the skipper again, so what the hell did it matter?

Liadain's information came back to his mind and, bruised about the heart though he was, he felt a stirring of purpose return. Perhaps he couldn't fight his own war any more, but in this world, could he still do his bit? The thought of resistance grew slowly, but as it did, the dragon's mouth opened slowly in a gape of moonstone teeth, and a wash of cool purple flame flickered about his ankles.

Ah. Yes, he thought, *good point.* Setting his foot in the angle of the dragon's elbow, then on the shoulder, he climbed up and took a seat on the long, sinuous back. It had what he considered to be the traditional arrangement of spikes all along its backbone, but when seen up close they were more like the humps of a camel, smooth knots of flesh beneath which the skin indented as it did in the hollows of a backbone. The result was a natural saddle, like that on a medieval warhorse, with a pommel before and cantle behind. A little tight for him, particularly in his boiler suit, flying jacket and Mae West, but smooth and not too hard, padded by a layer of fat.

The muscle worked beneath him, and he fell forward as the dragon brought its hind legs beneath itself. He grabbed at a dorsal spike to avoid being flung back again as it pushed up on its forelegs, walked with the awkward, deliberate tread of an iguana back to more solid ground. Sumala ran lightly up the trailing tail, followed by two guards, and as the dragon turned, bringing himself nose on into the wind, for all the world like a Lanc about to take flight, Oonagh jumped from ground to shoulder and set herself in the embroidered saddle.

I could kill her now, Flynn thought, separated only by the dragon's spike from her vulnerable back. His knife was still in his boot. A single stab and he could avenge the death of the boys. He could end Liadain's war at a stroke. These people at least could have peace.

With a swarming, uncomfortable run, the dragon hurled itself at the riverbank. It was higher here, two or three feet above the water's surface. The great muscles bunched and thrust. He scrabbled at the turf with claws as silver as moonlight, digging the point of his tail in and using it for extra thrust. The huge, membranous wings snapped out—the shape of his back changing beneath Flynn's seat. Flynn gripped with his knees as he'd been taught to do riding the carthorse on his uncle's farm, but the black scales gave no purchase, only a million reflections of himself, looking wild and wind tossed and a little fraught.

The river surface flattened in the down drop and pressure hammered Flynn into the ridge of spine. Tears came to his eyes. They rose in the air with a bound. Another down blast, and the dragon tucked its feet in close and, just missing the other bank of the river, began to laboriously climb the air as a man might climb a flight of steps. Every riser an effort.

Despite twenty-three operational sorties, Flynn didn't like to see the ground recede beneath him. He missed his navigator's cabin and the blackout curtains he could pull around him to shut out vision and fear. But he swallowed around the familiar smooth pebble of fear in his throat and looked down, memorising the lay of the land—river to waterfall,

waterfall to industrial heartland, distant glimmer of spaceships and mountains beyond. In the other direction the river bisected high moorlands and terminated in a lake ringed by tall hills and forest.

"Why didn't you tell me about the spaceships?" he asked, his hand heavy on his knee, as if he already carried the knife in his palm and was conscious of hiding it there.

"It is your destiny to do what you will do." Oonagh swung a leg about the pommel of her saddle, and used it to swivel, facing him. "Already there are signs that things are working out to my advantage. Is it my place to make your choices easier?"

"Yes, if I'm to be your champion."

"No. If that is what you are destined to be, that is what you will be." It was hard to tell what the thoughts were beneath the silver mirrors of her eyes, and her face was flawless and expressionless as a result. But her sigh was the sigh of a very old woman. "Yet if you have seen my country, you know why I must act. Your people are not the only ones fighting for their lives, Navigator. Tell me, do you like raining fire on the heads of innocent children? A warrior's honour is never to fight with drudges, serfs and women, and yet you go to war against all of these. Does your conscience not trouble you?"

He could have said yes. But not to her. "Not really. They bombed us first. Besides, Hitler has to be stopped. Gas chambers? Extermination camps? You can't compromise with that. Let them get rid of their madman, and we'll stop bombing, but there are worse things than dying, and having him win would be one."

"You would do anything to stop him."

"Almost."

"Then we understand each other, for I too am fighting against a future I will not allow to come to pass. You fight for your freedom. I fight for survival."

"Fine words." The slipstream blew bitterness out of Flynn's mouth. "And I've heard a lot of fine words recently. Which ones am I supposed to believe?"

She laughed, a full-throated, startling sound. "This is why I shall not give you any more words. If you are to be my champion, then my champion you will be, without persuasion or force."

"No force?" Sumala shouted into the wind, gesturing behind herself at the guards. "What do you call this?"

"Safeguarding my investment." Oonagh laughed again.

Beneath them, her merriment fell like rain on a pristine meadow. Between the mountains, the tallest thing in the plain lands was the hill of the palace, its crown as smoothly green as the pastureland, speckled with poppies and cornflowers. The slope of its sides looked bright as red flares, the lime wash reflecting the rosy light of sunlight. A processional line of standing stones wound up to the single great door, and the turf between them was smooth as any English bowling lawn. But where the river pushed its way back into daylight, the exit was concealed by a small copse of briars and elders.

There were other copses here and there in the meadow, making Flynn wonder if they concealed other exits. There was no reason, after all, why path upon path could not be threading through the darkness above and below the city's public streets.

"What do you intend to do with us?" Sumala asked, shouting over the woosh and rush of the wing beats and the shrill of all her bells.

"Nothing you need fear." Oonagh smiled. "It is important to me that your father should know I have not mistreated you."

Sumala's winglike black brows swept down over her almond-shaped eyes. She scowled very fetchingly, Flynn thought, and the thought had more weight than he might have liked. He could not go home, that much was certain. Therefore he must—if he was to live at all—learn to live with these people. It was probably allowable then to start noticing, once more, how very attractive the girl was.

Don't give up yet. We'll find you a way home.

His stomach was a snake pit, full of writhing cold. For the first time, he was sure his imaginary friend was lying. In any event, better treat life from now on as if he'd bailed out over occupied country. Better not to cling too hard to thoughts of what he'd lost—that way lay madness. Better think instead of what he might usefully achieve here.

He reconsidered his knife. The guards were behind Sumala. How quickly could they get to him? Quicker than he could bend down, draw the knife and stab it into Oonagh's back between the ribs?

Looking back, he met the gaze of the elf who had jabbed him earlier. This particular type affected red eyes, red hair and green skin. Ghastly! That and the intense stare, the look of personal affront he'd worn since he'd failed to lay Flynn out flat the first time, indicated a character who was waiting for the slightest opportunity to pounce.

Flynn leaned, got his fingers into his boot, and the shaft of the spear came down hard on his shoulder. The head of it, flickering with lime-sour light, stood out a little way from his chin. All the cells of his body cringed from the threat of the sting. He pushed the knife back into its scabbard and leaned away. Well, that answered that.

Through his clamped knees, he could feel the surge of a great heartbeat, and he wondered about the moment where he had seen the world through dragon eyes. What would it be like to bank and fly under your own power, in a grey world beneath a constant stream of tastes and scent? He could imagine it if he tried, but could not find words for the experience, even to describe it to himself.

Still, he could feel the jolt of impact from the landing through his own arms and legs, could almost imagine he felt the grate of soil and pebbles through his fingernails. He clung on tight as the great beast dug in, bracing itself against the sudden stop. When everything had settled enough for him to look up, he found its head swung towards him, an emotion that looked like laughter in the inferno of its eyes. Plumes of steam rose from its nostrils and glittered in the sunlight like a fountain of ruby.

Oonagh raised the deep hood of her cloak over her head before she leapt off. Her shadowed face disappeared, and only her jewels could be seen, glittering bloodlike in the radiance of the setting sun. It hung above the distant mountains like a shield of bronze, and the snow beneath it looked like gore.

Another zinging touch with the spear, and Flynn was beginning to get a little brassed off with his guard. But Sumala caught his wrist as he spun to take the creature down, shook her head. She pulled on the straps of his life jacket, bending his face down to hers. "Don't. You need to be conscious when they put you on the slab. It won't work, otherwise." And he thought that since he had decided he was trusting her, he might as well carry on doing it.

Subsiding, he watched the dragon swarm down the side of the hill like a gecko on a wall, headfirst, disappearing into the front gate, scattering passersby as it went. He and Sumala were escorted across the top of the mound to where a toppled monolith lay covered with worms of carving. Oonagh spoke to it,

19

and its shadow became a stairway, leading down by private ways into the blue underground light of the city.

The escort of soldiers closed in about the queen and drove Flynn and Sumala before them through empty passages. No one to mark their queen's passing, to bow or fawn, or offer violence. The idea of her sneaking through her secret tunnels, far away from the gaze of her subjects, did not count in her favour with Flynn. But perhaps she too knew of the resistance, and was afraid.

His musings ended when he found himself once again in the prison of the sleepers. When he was prodded to lie down on one of the stone tables, his misery and resignation evaporated. This eternal sleep looked too much like death. Sod just lying there and taking it! He panicked, put his head down and charged at the guards, got in a couple of solid hits, a fierce delight in being able to do *something* fizzing in his veins.

He tasted bitterness, like lemon drops in the back of his throat, as Ghastly dinged him a glancing blow with his cattle prod of a weapon. Grabbing the spear, he wrested it from Ghastly's hands, caught the elf beneath the ribs with the butt of it. And was just swinging it round to bring the head to bear when Sumala stepped to his side, avoided his flailing arms with ease and pressed a spot at the centre of his biceps. The scalding pain was followed immediately by numbness. His hand opened by itself, and with a rapid twist and wriggle he could barely see for its speed, Ghastly pulled his spear back and gave Flynn one more shot of tooth-jangling pain.

"Oh, bad show!" Flynn cried, looking at Sumala with disappointment and no small betrayal as five of them seized his arms and legs and forced him to lie down flat on the table. There was a feeling of pressure, struggle. He saw the arch of the ceiling above, laced with grey stars.

...and then he slowly became aware of his den around him, the slip and slither of rounded golden pebbles beneath him, smooth as water-tumbled cobbles. He tasted oil and meat, and the blood-copper tang of the lines of malachite in the distant walls. Closer to him, the stink of eagles, guano and gore and their incessantly cheeping chicks. Lazily, he extended his snout and butted the bars that separated their nests from his. "Keep the noise down!"

He stretched out a claw and examined it in the dim of the cavern. Yes, still his claw, adamant tipped and sharp. When he flickered out his tongue he could taste only birds and gold, all the usual presences of his off-time world. But had he really said "Keep the noise down" like a father of toddlers to a rabble of urchins in the street?

He sniffed again, tasted the floor to see if he could scent the faint savour of footsteps, and someone—he was sure it wasn't him—giggled. A flick of ears detected no unknown breathing in the vicinity. The eagle chicks were waiting for their hourly ration of bull carcasses and had not matured enough to speak. He'd never known an eagle to giggle, in any case.

Wait, he thought, picking up his claws and touching his face with them, poking himself in the nostril and then the eye. *Where are my hands?*

The giggle came again, and with all his senses on alert, he was aware, this time, that it came from within the depths of his own mind. "Silly. They're on the slab with the rest of you, in the room of sleepers."

He uncurled his bulk and scrabbled out of the bowl of his den—the bowl lined with gold. Dragging himself to the door, he squeezed beneath the lintel into the main tack house. Servants bowed and averted their gazes, covering their eyes as they would have done for the queen.

Curse her.

There was no one here who would have giggled. No one here who even knew of the room of sleepers. But the fleeting moment of malice towards Oonagh echoed strangely in the caverns of his mind, as if it reflected from more than one mirror.

He closed his eyes, concentrated. "Sumala, is that you?"

"Of course it is. It's both of us."

Setting his chin in the entrance of the city, so that the stream of business must climb over his nose, Kanath amused himself by people-watching, smelling a thousand different varieties of fear and resolve. "This happened when you looked at me," he hazarded. "Before you mounted. You looked in my eye. This happened then."

"I'm sorry!" A female voice came with memories of splendour, of green woodlands hot with the smell of hibiscus, tall slopes leading up to snow, of prayer flags and trumpets, chariots and elephants and drums. Its apology was unconvincing—it felt it had every right to act as it had done, and beneath the righteous certainty, it also felt very pleased with its own cleverness.

"What have you done?" Kanath asked, though he could smell them, now he knew, smell them on his back and his harness, and trace that smell down the spiral winds of the city to the still place just below the heart, where time was siphoned away from the ne'er-do-wells and criminals of the city to go towards Oonagh's projects. "How is time passing for you at all?"

"You have a splinter of my soul in you," replied the female voice smugly. "And the soul is eternal and beyond time. All things happen to it at once. It creates the illusion of past and present to make sense of the tangle, but it is outside the threads. The people of your world seem very capable of manipulating time, dragon, it is sad that they know nothing about what they meddle with."

At the conversation, feeling the difference between the bright, innocent naivety of Sumala's presence and the age-worn weariness of the dragon, Flynn managed to locate enough of his own mind to differentiate himself from the others. "You did the same to me," he thought, and his mental voice sounded worried to himself, anxious and tired. Their mutual fatigue gave him a strange cross-species sympathy for the dragon. "Does that hurt? How many times can you do it before there's nothing left?"

"Silly." Sumala's smile coloured her mind electric blue. "The soul is like time—it can be divided infinitely, and each part will be whole. All my people can do this, easy as breathing. If I had not done it to you, you would be still suspended in the moment when you lay down. You'd know nothing else until you woke, perhaps a thousand years into the future, and experienced one bright flash of death before becoming part of the dust on the sleepers' floor.

"This is the way I helped you to come and rescue me, teaching you how to work the controls when you should have known nothing. You weren't aware of me, but I was there. One cannot, though, sneak into a dragon's mind unobserved. I think you helped us, Kanath. I think you want to help us more."

He roused again, straightened his aching legs and crawled along the pleasant scratch of the main road, out into the night. Above, the night sky looked exactly like the vault of the sleepers' chamber, grey stars and two grey moons hanging over a grey land. The air tasted of burrowing things, worms come up to peek at the surface, night-hunting birds and the gold-green-blue outpouring of hot scents from beneath the hill.

"Want to help you?" Kanath paced up the ramp to the top of the hill, and this time Flynn got to feel the takeoff from inside—the burst of energy and effort, the painful haul, the drop from the edge of the mound and the air beneath his wings like water beneath the arms of a swimmer. There was no more exhilaration than there would be for a man setting out for a walk, and Flynn felt, on the whole, that being inside a Lanc was a better deal. "Why should I desire to help you?"

Good question. "Well," said Sumala, an edge of uncertainty in her mental tone, "because you do not like being a beast of burden. Because you are proud and free and no pet."

"I am no pet."

"Because," Flynn hazarded, "you don't seem to be fighting this. I can't say I was keen on walking around with someone else's soul inside me, but you seem to have taken to it like a natural."

"You wish me to resist you? I could snap my mind like my teeth, chew you both and swallow you."

In their shared belly, Flynn felt fire roil—literal fire, the tongues of it tickling pleasantly. Kanath rumbled and a wash of brimstone-tasting smoke lapped up his throat. Flynn tried to make him blow smoke rings, but his grasp on the body had become slippery. He'd raised the claw with no difficulty, before, but now Kanath knew what was happening, he had restored his ownership with so little fuss Flynn had not noticed it happening. He breathed out a jet of flame, in what Flynn could feel was laughter.

"Not at all. But if you felt like helping us...?"

All this time the dragon's steady wing beats had been driving it upwards, straight towards the larger of the two moons. The stars had become very bright as they burst through thin films of icing cloud, looked down on the haze of atmosphere, and the palace and grounds. It was possible to see the edges now, to see they had come from a worldlet whose roots dangled into nothingness.

Kanath took one last breath of depleted air and closed his nostrils. Another wing beat and a surge forward, and he breached the outer layer of air, sailed out into space. His scales clamped tight, forming a natural pressure suit, and the fires inside warmed him against the utter cold. The weightlessness was as soothing as a bath for a moment, before he had caught the lip of the closest moon's gravity well and was using it to fling himself past, and out through the x-rays and the violet scent of the solar wind.

This closest moon was shaped into a rough pyramid and covered on all sides with fields. A continent of vineyards, an archipelago of orchards, and three-sided fields the size of countries, burgeoning with other crops. Obligingly, Kanath focussed—he had long sight that would put a hawk to shame—and Flynn saw the figures toiling in the fields, wondered what it was about them that looked familiar.

"They are human slaves."

"Oh."

Coming out from beneath the bulk of the harvest moonlet, they swam up towards the second moon, which proved on closer examination to be a huge, blasted world. They dived into its arid air, and though everything Kanath saw was monochrome, this place smelled grey. As up became down, Flynn saw the dejected shapes of a city below. Laid out like the palace, around a road that was a single spiral, it looked at first like a dropped shell buried in black sand.

Kanath swept down and landed on the cracked pavement of the central avenue in a district where stone amphitheatres gave way to lumpy cairns. They gleamed fitfully as the scouring

25

breeze removed a layer of dust only to replace it with another, and Flynn saw they were made up of swords, arrowheads, spears, pile upon pile, surfaces constantly abraded by the wind, rubbed blunt but shining.

"What on earth?"

No reply from Kanath, only a reverent sadness, such as a man might feel when he walked among graves.

"I think they are sacrifices," Sumala said, her mental voice hushed. "I think this city is a temple. You see down there? Hostelries for the pilgrims, baths where they can clean themselves. A place to give up their weapons. It is a temple of peace, I think, but the god has left it."

"Or she is dead," Kanath acknowledged. He had come out from among the abandoned piles of blades and now he left the road, turning right into a mausoleum of crumbling sculptures. A crushing weariness built up in Flynn with every inchoate shape.

Incense, gold, blue, like a smell of firecrackers, and Kanath's head swung round, sniffing. Once he had stopped moving, the wind coated him in dust, made him indistinguishable from the ruins—a statue of a dragon. But, inside, all three of them had leapt a little for joy.

The centre of the city was three massive buildings arranged around a parade square. Each building trailed a curved tail of small shrines, so that—observed from the air—the effect was of a three-legged wheel. All were decrepit and empty except for the small shrine closest to them. There, a candle-lantern's wax-warm light flickered. When Kanath peered, they could see, through the windows, an undamaged statue of a woman in a carriage of living wood, driving on her team of spotted panthers. There were flowers at her feet and a black bundle of something that slowly unfolded itself from its crouch and became a young priest with his eyes closed and his fingers smudged with pollen.

Kanath looked away, and Flynn was glad of it. It seemed intrusive to stare at the poor creature, left alone in his pieties in the middle of ruin.

"My father said Oonagh's people were once like ours," Sumala offered gently. "Glad to make music and dance before the gods. But they lost their gods and we did not. It is a terrible thing, my father said, to be suddenly without the purpose for which you were made."

Scent came like a shout streaming past them from the central square, the taste of bronze and elf-flesh with its almost chlorophyll-like tang. Kanath swarmed forwards until he could put his snout around the final statue and look. There was a rumbling and a shudder beneath his feet, and from the broken doorway of the farthest temple elvish figures began to emerge. A batch of nine came sauntering into the dusty air, drew themselves up into a ragged line, and as they were doing so another nine emerged, and then another.

Barracks underground, Flynn thought, *and some kind of lift to the surface. They're coming out for a bit of square bashing? They bloody need to, they're an absolute shambles.*

He counted eighty-one groups of nine soldiers, and then a group of three, all of them in chain mail except the last. "Why are you showing me this?"

Kanath's fire leapt, filling him with warmth. "Show you things? I am merely out for my evening's exercise."

"Where's the army to be sent?"

The blaze grew so hot it scorched him. "How am I to know? Shall we look?"

The scratching of his claws blown away by the ever-present shrill of the sandstorm, his nostrils and eyes slitted, the dragon writhed like a great lizard out from the shelter of the garden of statues into something that must once have been parkland, if the dust-filled flowerbeds and dead trees were any indication. He reached the terrace of shrines and, digging his claws into the stone, swarmed slowly up to lie along the flat roof like a carving.

The last three elves of the host were now lying down on couches set around an ornamental pond in the centre of the parade square. With a flash that turned the swirling dust clouds into bright white veils, the waters lit up, mirror smooth, mirror bright. When Kanath looked through, they could see farmland beneath clear skies dotted with cloud. A tractor in the distance and, closer to them, a man in overall trousers and a checked shirt, bending down to rub behind the ears of his mongrel dog.

Flynn's body rested in timeless suspension back at the palace. Without it—without moist palms, the plunge of his stomach, the halt and race of his heart—he could muster only an intellectual horror. But that was bad enough. "I was told Oonagh meant to attack Sumala's people. Not mine!"

"She will have to go through your world to get to mine," Sumala said, a note of strained patience in her tone, as if she had expected him to have grasped this earlier. "And she will not wish to move her armies through hostile territory. It is only good tactics for her to capture your world first, in order to get to mine. I thought that should be clear even to you."

There was no body to provide the panic and the sickness, but no sickness and panic to distract him from the ramifications. *This* was why he was here in Elfland, then. Not for Oonagh's prophecy, and not due to some cosmic mistake. No, he'd obviously been placed here to stop this, providentially given the chance to save his world. It was the war, writ large over the universe. What point defeating Hitler if the world was only to go down beneath an even more inhuman regime?

"Take us back, Kanath. Now!"

"Uninvited guests should be more polite," remarked the dragon casually. The three-way whole of them, which had begun to feel almost comfortable, wavered as a dark-shining mass bulged beneath it and burst. Flynn's grasp on himself exploded into flying droplets. He grabbed for them and they ran through his mental fingers. He was three people at once, and none at all. He was desolate and resentful at his father's inaction, satisfied over his triumph as he would have been over the sweet taste of a mouthful of gold.

Something in Flynn, impatient and certain, thought, *No. I don't have time to lose myself like this,* and began to plot the coordinates of himself on his own mental map. Here was his ego, here his memories of RAF training, here a cloistered and lonely childhood, and here his mental skipper, revealed as three parts wishful thinking and one part need.

The skipper had his insubstantial foot on a thing that looked like a horizontal silver tree. Lightning moved up it and down again, bathing it in an eerie blue light. "Give this a kick," he said. "Tell your young woman to do the same."

"She's not my…" he began, guiltily, and then stopped as his priorities rearranged themselves. "I need your help. Not yours—you're just a figment of my imagination. I need the real man. He'll know what to do. I've got to let him know."

Sumala's dance-toughened foot kicked the silver thing so hard that pain went through Flynn's head like a needle. But the pain subsided faster for him than it did for the dragon. When she did it again, he used that moment of grace from Kanath's will to reconnect all his severed parts into one personality. He could feel the graze on his jaw as Kanath whipped his head from side to side, trying to shake out the agony.

The landscape of his mind bulged and distorted, and Flynn felt the pressure of the beast's will come against him like a flying cloud of ash. He resisted being pulled apart again, resisted the sting and scour and increasing agony. Wished for a body so he might double over, sob 'til his nose streamed blood and the pressure drove blood out of his tear ducts and his burst ears. But he had no body to either suffer or fail, no prospect of relief by lapsing into unconsciousness. Instead, he pictured himself pushing his way forward through the blast of will, kneeling on the tree—it looked now like a stream with many tributaries, all of them flickering with electrical impulses, and he understood suddenly that it was a nerve ganglion in the dragon's brain, one that, activated, caused him agony.

He pictured himself pulling the knife from his boot and jabbing it down where the fibres were most tangled, watching the pulse of darkness follow the wound, laughing in the strange blazing ecstasy of the pain.

"Stop it!" Kanath writhed on the derelict roof, trying to bury his head in the cold dirt to get some relief from the stabbing ache. He rolled onto his back, felt the lip of the roof too late and fell, flailing, into the narrow street in front of the shrines. Dust broke his fall, fountained up all around him, and the wind whisked it away with a hiss.

The fall shocked them into an uneasy truce, for long enough, at least, to notice how the light had changed. Kanath heaved over and got his feet back on the ground. His jaw landed with a muffled thud on the street and, as he was pawing at his sore muzzle, he opened his eyes and saw, through the bracket of his claws, the priest of the shrine, lantern held high, watching him with mingled wariness and concern.

The idea struck Flynn readymade. One of his rare moments of inspiration. "Sumala, quick, put a piece of your soul in him. Tell him he has to warn the skipper about the invasion. Tell him I said 'remember Doncaster'. You're pretty much divine already, he'll think it's a message from his goddess. He'll be glad."

"Have I not done enough for you already? I want out. I want to go home."

"Please. If Skip can stop her getting through my world, then she won't ever get to yours. You'll still have a home to go to. Sumala!"

"Very well."

Kanath was already looking at the man. Close to, one could see he was not young at all. Age had piled up in his gaze like the dust on his world. Out of the corner of Flynn's mental eye, he thought he caught a glimpse of something golden, glittering, that passed like a comet's tail along the locked gazes. Then the priest frowned, shook himself as if from a sleep, and picked up a conversation Flynn had not been aware they had been having.

"No, windlord. I am too old for the vanity of war. I cannot tell you what you ask. I have not paid attention to anything beyond these four walls for a thousand years."

Kanath's disgust was like a red itch beneath the skin. "Go back to your dead god, then, priest, entombed in your mausoleum. You have been no help to the living, lo, this millennium, why should you start now?"

The dragon paced back into the garden of sculptures, found the highest and climbed it, his claws leaving gouges in the undefined shape. There might have been a crown on the head where he perched for a moment, getting his breath back. Then he tossed himself out into the streamers of dust. The great wings snapped out, caught the wind, and he allowed himself to be swept away like a kite with a cut string.

This time the journey through space passed slowly enough for the dragon to begin to feel the burn of oxygen deprivation in his muscles, the maddening urge to breathe. When they reached the ground, Flynn felt as wrung out as if he'd just put down after a twelve-hour flight over Happy Valley. He knew the feel of a joyride well enough, and that—that had not been it.

"Look, Kanath. I apologise for being rude and for causing you pain. But you showed us that for a reason, yes? Help us now. Help us to get free so that we can do something about it."

"He's Oonagh's dog, after all." Sumala's tone was grim. "He showed us this just to make us sad, because he thinks we are powerless."

She slipped through the loom of consciousness and tugged on the threads that moved the dragon's head, pointing him at the palace, at the waterway entrance through which Flynn had sailed to save her. "Go there!"

Kanath grumbled but obeyed, landing in the stream, swimming like a huge black crocodile into the darkness.

This time they passed boats coming in the opposite direction, watched the boatmen cover their eyes and look away. The scent of fear was like frankincense. It made Flynn think of Sunday service and quieted Kanath almost in the same way. "I am no dog. I am a god," he said.

Hauling himself out of the water at the landing place, he shook himself and was for one moment surrounded by flying diamonds of blue-lit drops. Then he writhed up to the stairs and put his head in the arch of the first spiral of the stairs. A certain smugness had now come back into his thoughts.

"Go on!" Sumala kicked out again, the jab of pain uniting with Flynn's sudden realisation of the truth. He rode along and felt the jolt of cold stone against his own shoulders as Kanath tried to squeeze into the hole. It was far too small for him.

"And the stair down to the sleepers from the Gate of Will is smaller." Flynn reached out to soothe with his imaginary hand the place they had battered between them. The flow of current rejoined itself seamlessly, and Kanath raised his head higher, put up the ridge of his back as a crest and gave a full-body shake.

"Exactly," he said. "I cannot because I cannot. You should have chosen another host, my parasite friends. I cannot free you from your prison. No matter how you torment me, I cannot reunite you with your bodies. So now the question is, do I let you stay on whole in my mind, or do I pull you into such tiny pieces you will never come together again?

"Fee fi fo fum, I smell the soul of an Englishman. Be he alive or be he dead, I'll grind his mind until it's fled." He laughed with a burst of purple flame. "What do you say to that then, you who dared to command the windlord of a queen?"

Chapter Two

"Need to talk to you, Padre." Chris thumbed his phone open and shut, watching as the reflection of the stained-glass window was deflected up to hit one of the angels of the roof beams square in the face. A service of baptism had just finished, the proud parents and godparents departed, and Grace, in full ecclesiastical vestments, was putting out the candles and smoothing the cloth that covered the altar.

She smiled to see him, though it was a smile with a touch of exasperation. "All right. But you can turn that thing off and put it away. You're in the house of God, nothing more important than that is going to happen while you're here."

With a little laugh, he switched the phone off and tucked it into his back pocket. "It's a deal. Grace, I want to talk to you about—"

"Just one moment." She finished her tidying up, pulling a small plug out of the font and wiping it dry with a linen cloth that she passed to a beaming child in a surplice. Chris made his way into the Lady Chapel, where a modern-art Mary, looking like an Isle of Arran chessman, sat in front of the mutilated remains of an earlier statue. Evidently the queen of heaven was making a cautious comeback now the iconoclastic passion of the more zealous kind of Protestant had been tamed.

For lack of something to do, and for luck, he put 20p in the collection box and lit a candle, standing it upright in the sandy tray in front of her niche. The light was calming, still and upright, golden as the summer morning outside.

"So." Grace returned to sit next to him on one of the modern upholstered chairs. She had taken off the gorgeous green silk and the floor-length snowy linen of her vestments, and was now resplendent in a ragged skirt, tie-died T-shirt and a pair of Doc Martens. "Tell me what's on your mind."

Easier said than done. Chris picked up one of the meditation stones that had considerately been placed nearby, next to a rack of leaflets on new and trendy ways to pray. "I think Geoff's alive."

Grace crossed her legs at the ankle and leaned forward, intent. "The Geoff you told me about? The one..."

"My lover, yes."

She looked startled, a little offended, but he didn't have time to play games. She'd brought this out into the open herself, now let her deal with it. "To be more specific, I think he's alive and a prisoner in Faerie. Tell me how I can get him back."

Grace lit her own candle and pondered it. The flame picked out the lines of her frown in gilding. "Why do you assume that I know?"

"Because this is your job, Padre—the supernatural. If you don't know, you can find out. I want him back, and I don't care what it takes."

Her sigh echoed in the tall, empty room. "Yes. That's why I worry." She raised a hand to forestall his protest. "No, don't say anything. I know all the arguments. I just wish you weren't going up against *them* while you are in such a morally fragile place."

35

"Bollocks, Padre." Chris leapt to his feet, instantly enraged at the silence, the dim sepulchral loftiness of the room, the cross on the far altar and even the light streaming through the stained-glass saints. "I could go down the road to St. Andrews right now and find a priest there who'd be glad to marry me to Ben or Geoff, bishops' guidance notwithstanding. Don't try and tell me you're the only one who's got the inside gen on this. The church is practising a Christian charity it doesn't preach, and I'm all for that. If you're going to be a hypocrite, you ought to do it that way around. I'd still rather you weren't a hypocrite at all."

Grace stood too, her mouth gone hard, her pink hair looking ridiculously festive atop an expression that promised hellfire. "Don't call me a hypocrite, Chris. You know I believe what I believe, and I've never claimed anything else."

"I didn't come in here to argue theology."

"Why *did* you come?"

He considered for a moment taking one of the meditation stones and throwing it through a glass angel's wing. But the colour was so beautiful, the painting so subtle, a master craftsman's heart and soul had gone into it, and he couldn't. He couldn't even hold on to the anger. She believed what she'd been taught, so had he, not so long ago.

He sighed, sat down. "I came for help."

At his surrender, Grace softened. She perched on the edge of her chair and gave a quiet laugh. "You have such a way of asking for it, Chris. But then I've always known that. I shouldn't let you rile me up. I'm sorry."

Chris spoke to his joined hands, wedged beneath his knees where they could not betray him by trembling. "I know it's been fifteen years. Nearly seventy years, even. I just want it dealt with *now*. I hate the waiting."

"I hate"—Grace gave a little laugh—"that my church doesn't seem to know what to believe any more. I know God's there—I can feel him—and that should be important. Yes? Yet we're bickering over gay rights the same way we bickered over women priests. It should be obvious—the answer should be obvious. The way should be lit, so that we know how to follow it. And it isn't, and I don't know why not."

"Crisis of faith, eh?"

"No." She laughed again with a little more heart to it. "Or not at least in Jesus. But in the church, yes. And it makes me sad. My father always says that in Nigeria we preserved the faith as it was handed to us. Those who came and taught it claimed that they knew the answers to everything. But now it seems that they were lying about that too, he says. We have kept it alive the way it was handed to us, and in the meantime, in the home church, they were falling away—or rising up—and leaving us behind. And now you expect us once more to do things your way, even though you keep changing your mind."

Chris reached out and picked up the stone again, rubbing it. It was soothing, strangely enough. "Who's 'you' in this context?" he ventured at last.

Grace shook her head. "Don't mind me. It's a shock, I suppose. I thought we were agreed about this, you and I. It was a comfort. Now I'm not sure what to think."

"Okay, I'll tell you what I think about your problem. Then you give me the gen on mine, okay?"

She tilted her head, he took that as a yes.

"When you can stop a teenage boy from thinking about sex every five minutes, then you can talk to me about 'it's not your fault how you were made, it's all about how you act'. That's bollocks too, as Jesus knew perfectly well. Guy who looks with lust at a girl—just as guilty as the one who lies with her. So don't try to give me that middle-of-the-road clever little compromise. It doesn't work. What I do or don't do, being gay is what I *am*. And if that's abominable, then *I'm* abominable. Hate the sin but love the sinner isn't possible in these circs. I *am* the sin."

This was not what he'd come in for, but there was something undeniably satisfying about saying it aloud. Here of all places, where the sunlight nesting amid the rafters was blue with incense, and the silence had a quality suggesting a listening ear. "So, Grace, you'd better decide now what you really think. Am I deserving of eternal punishment because I was once in love with the bravest, though the most indecisive lad you ever did see? If Him up above opened up the furnaces right now, would you throw me in?"

She looked insulted. "Of course not!"

And he swallowed a little feeling of relief. One friendship saved at least. On shaky foundations still, but with hope of improvement later. "Glad to hear it. D'you think God's more or less merciful than you?"

"All right." She got up, jerked her chin towards the back of the church, where, behind carved ash doors, a small kitchen was hidden. "You've made your point. Feeling the thirst after righteousness? Shall I put the kettle on?"

"I could do with something." Tea, as usual, calmed the friction, brought order back into a frayed world. "Got any biscuits?"

With a mug and a chocolate digestive in hand, they opened the nave door and sat on the worn flagstones together, looking out at the graveyard, which was clad in trumpets of bindweed and shaggy with long grass that was turning champagne blond in the long hot summer without rain.

"So," he said, eventually, "any ideas?"

Grace twitched as her expression of deep thought passed through bemusement—catching up with the change of subject—and then into wariness. "I'd suggest prayer, but I know you're not a praying man."

"I've been known to shriek for help from the Almighty now and again. But I agree it's not something I should do in the main course of things."

"To get someone out from Faerie you need magic. Strong magic. I don't know whether it can be done without an unshakeable faith in *something*." She propped her chin on her curled hand and contemplated the toes of her boots. The scuffed red leather looked in the sunshine like ruby slippers—if slippers had calf-high lacing and extreme grip, kick-ass, black rubber soles.

"Do you have an unshakeable faith in anything, Chris?"

He thought immediately of Geoff. Geoff who always knew which way to turn, which way would lead him home. Lost in a white shrouded world of nothingness, flying on artificial horizon and compass, with half an hour's fuel and no idea where England lay, he'd say, "Navigator, can I have a course," and the coordinates would come back before he had time to breathe. But Geoff—well he was obviously bloody trying, but he was equally obviously failing to find a way back here, and if *he* didn't know, then what else was there?

"Beer and cigarettes?"

"Don't be facetious." Grace rooted around in the cutlery drawer and then the pile of hassocks, emerging with a triumphant "Ha!" and a small red pot of saccharine tablets. "I'm thinking about sacraments. A sacrament is a physical thing which represents and focuses a spiritual power. I could give you holy water. I could even give you the Host—I trust you that much. But could you really be resigned enough to God's will to allow Him to work through them effectively? To work through you effectively. I don't know that you trust Him enough."

"I don't know that you do either, Padre."

"No," she said, smiling. "That's why there are so few miracles these days. It's hard to give up power entirely without knowing the outcome first."

A sparrow flew from the yew trees of the churchyard into the carven boughs of the church. Chris had a strange flash of sympathy for it, imagining hot little feet on cool stone, delicious shade, welcome after all that glare.

"So," Grace continued, "Faerie is a spiritual realm, not a physical one. Its laws are responsive to your willpower. What you need, to force a way in, is to find something which works as a sacrament for you." She steepled her fingers and pressed them to her lips. "Something which helps you to realise your own strength, which enables you to connect your will to your ability to use it. Does that help?"

"Such as?"

"I don't know! It's a personal thing—I don't know better than you do what's likely to unlock the inner recesses of your soul. The MPA logo, maybe? That stands for everything we've been doing these past three years. We've seen off our fair share of paranormal beasties, and the MPA was always your baby. How about that?"

Chris imagined himself sewing the logo onto his shirt, going into battle with it on his chest, like a long-winded Superman. "I'll have a think about it."

"Do." She put her palms behind her on the warm flagged floor and stretched. "And I'll have a think about what you said too."

The sky slowly clouded over as Chris walked home, along roads clogged with tourists and ramblers. Unhappy red faces all around him, for the grey clouds seemed to trap the heat. The roads sweltered as in an oven. Far off, over Matlock Peak, darker grey clouds held thunder, and the world seemed to crouch down, breathless, sticky, waiting for the rain.

The downpour had started as he opened his front door, switched on the computer and moved into the kitchen to give it time to boot. By the time he had filled the kettle, rain was tapping like fingers on the window. The light continued to fail, and when he stood by the sink and looked out, a sense of wrongness niggled him. Something was up. But the distant hillsides looked dour and calm as ever. Something in the garden, then? He focussed on the forlorn shapes of the engines he had taken apart to see how they worked and not quite managed to put back together. But they were as rusty and disheartened as ever in their tangles of quick-growing roses and pennyroyal.

Still something flickered, just out of sight. He stepped back, and there it was—in every droplet of water that ran down the windows was a face, and every face the same, all of them vainly mouthing soundless phrases at him.

"Geoff?"

But it wasn't Geoff. He grabbed a soup bowl from the draining rack, wrestled with the back door and ran out into the deluge, holding out the bowl and catching the falling water. All the faces ran into one as he did so, and candlelight wavered up from the bowl and spilled over his hands.

He could see the face much clearer now—round, earnest, flawless, with plump pink lips like flower petals and milky, ancient eyes. At the same time, he knew he had been seen—the creature stopped talking, lowered the hood from around his head and showed hair brown as good soil, and on it a circlet shaped like a two-headed serpent. When he shook his wrists free of the cloak, they too were gauntleted to the elbow with golden snakes.

A badge of office of some kind, Chris thought. *He expects me to recognise what he is.* But he didn't know the secret handshake, so he forced himself to smile.

It seemed to do the trick. The monk or priest, or whatever he was, unrolled a scroll and held it out for Chris to read. In beautiful calligraphy, around which someone had clearly spent hours drawing and painting small birds, it said, *He says you must be told there is an invasion coming. He has seen the troops himself, arrayed for battle and awaiting the command.*

Oh shit. Chris stopped admiring the scroll, bit down on the automatic protest, the cry of *Fucking hell! What do you expect me to do about it?* That he knew was just the helpless anger born out of fear.

He does not know when nor where they will come. But so that you may know it is he who sends these words, he bids you remember Doncaster.

Geoff! Geoff was the only one in any world who could have sent that message. Chris patted himself down frantically but came up empty handed. No pen or paper. He dashed back inside, found the pad by the phone and wrote *Where is he? Is he okay?* Ran back out and found only a bowl full of rain, cold and grey. He flung it at the wall, felt no better when it smashed and the shards disappeared into the tangle of undergrowth.

Back to the kettle. He made himself a cup of tea, drank it, got the panic back under its cap and welded it as tight as he could manage. Still felt a little sick but that could be borne. The important thing was to take appropriate action, and getting into Faerie had never looked more vital. Back to the plan, then, just with a higher degree of urgency.

A place of power, hey? A physical reminder of his will, something with which he could change the world? Oh yes, there once had been something of that kind. Half an hour's googling pulled out the information that there still was, away on the other side of the Peaks. In Langdale, the Museum of Aviation History housed one of the only complete Mosquitoes left. They were working on it even now, trying to restore it to join the Battle of Britain flight. The Andrews Sisters warbled tinnily out of his computer speakers as he read, provoking a rush of calm as the learned habits of wartime reasserted themselves.

The website which claimed that the plane was nearly complete was itself a year old and had not been updated in all that time. He leaned back in his seat and looked at the picture. There wasn't a plane like it. The Spitfire boys got all the glory, but he doubted if there was anyone left on the planet who could do what he could do with a bombed-up Mosquito.

He wrote down the phone number on a pad of paper, looked for the house phone, which he seemed to have left somewhere again. Bloody hell. By now it would probably have gone flat and need recharging before use. Why they didn't keep them attached to cords any more, he didn't know. At least you didn't wander off with the receiver and lose it somewhere when it was screwed to the wall.

Taking his mobile from his trouser pocket, he switched it back on. Two messages, just in the short time he'd been incommunicado. He turned down the computer speaker with a huff of annoyance and played the first one. Stan's number and Stan's father saying, "I want a word with you, Mr. Gatrell. Don't try pretending you haven't got this message. I'll know when you pick it up, so don't try weaselling out of it."

Extraordinary. He phoned Stan's number at once and shifted in his seat as suppressed anger made his spine itch. He really did not have time for this today.

43

"Hello, Fred Grimshore here. Who's that?"

"Mr. Gatrell. You asked me to call."

The voice on the other end deepened almost a full octave into a growl. "Oh, it's you, is it?"

"Of course it is. You asked me to call. What is this..."

"Why the fuck did you give my boy fifty quid?"

Chris's mind was still a long way away, in the 1940s. He didn't immediately see what was so wrong in helping a boy to develop his talent and in paying him a fair price for the components and labour he had put in on a project that benefited them both. "He's been doing some work for me," he said, unsettled by the man's attitude. "Is there something wrong with that?"

"What kind of work?"

"It's complicated." Chris shrugged, noticed that his tea had gone cold and that the second message was from Ben. How was Ben, anyway, this first day back at work? Perhaps he should have checked? "Some...er...image processing."

"You what?" The growl roughened. Malice could practically be seen, dripping off the sliver finish of the phone onto the floor, shimmering over it like a haze. Unprepared, Chris felt the hostility like a blow to the chest. "Pictures? What kind of pictures?"

He had a suspicion that the truth might not go down well, but what else was there? "Ghosts, mostly. Some elves, but they're tricky—don't come out well on any kind of film."

"You fucking loony! Listen, I heard from our Karen at the Red Lion you'd started seeing things. Acting crazy. So I ask my son what he does with your lot and he looks shifty, and I find he's got fifty quid from you stashed under the bed. You get my drift? So I'll tell you what's going to happen now. You get lost.

You never talk to him again, you never come round here ever again. 'Cause if you do, I'll fucking murder you, and I'm not kidding. I've got a spade and a patch in the garden marked out for you. All right?"

"It most certainly is not—" The phone cut off. "All right," Chris finished, watching sparkly stars dance on the computer screen, advertising online poker. A chance to lose money without all this recrimination. He swallowed, something in his belly tying itself up in a knot. What on earth was that about? Sometimes he thought it was the entire world that had gone mad, not him at all. Bloody man, no wonder Stan was shy and something of a sneak, living with a father who reacted like that to a friendly stranger offering encouragement.

He called up Google maps and worked out how long it would take to drive to Langdale. A little over two hours. Not bad at all. Maybe he'd do it now, offer a knowledgeable eye or a test pilot's experience. The threat of invasion surely trumped any other priorities he might have.

But the message from Ben remained unanswered. He watched the phone for a moment, trying to guess whether it would be good or bad news, and a little warmth stirred just under his breastbone and untangled some of his anger and anxiety. He realised he was holding the message in the palm of his hand for all the world as if it too were a sacrament, a talisman. But it wasn't. It was only a phone call.

He hit *Listen*, anticipating the sound of Ben's voice, the irreverent and glorious strength of it. The boy would have made a good flight engineer. Always calm, always thinking ahead. He knew how not to show fear, even when it was eating him up. He'd have done all right in a Lanc.

Chris was caught with a smile on his face when the first words tumbled out. "Fuck you! Damn you to hell, Chris. What the fuck are you doing? Oh please!" The saw of terrified breathing mixed with sobs.

"There was a thing at the office. It was going for a... It was going for a customer. I had to use the vial—the water—to get rid of it. I thought I'd run to the Red Lion, but now I don't know where I am. There's nothing outside the car. It's all just white. I'm s-scared, Chris. I don't know what to do. Shit! There's something out there."

Chris was already out of the front door, scrabbling in his pocket for his keys. They snagged on the inside of his pocket, tore, and Ben said, "Chris! Chris, where the fucking hell are you?"

"Hey, hey." He got the car door open, the key in the ignition. "It's all right, just hold on, I'm coming. I'll be there in no time. Where are you?"

"You promised not to let this happen to me. You promised!"

Chris looked helplessly at the phone. For a moment he'd forgotten it was just a recording, half an hour old. Whatever was going to happen had already happened, and despite his fine words, he had not been there. He'd been looking up old planes on the internet and thinking of Geoff.

"Help me." Ben's words were all but indistinguishable beneath the choke of tears and terror. "No. Chris. Help me! Help me. No!"

A rending noise, like a falling wall—like a steel door being torn down—and then a click. Silence. Chris thought for a moment he could hear something residual on the line, realised it was his own speeding breath. He felt nauseous with adrenaline, and his hands shook so much he dropped the phone into the footwell as he tried to put it away.

Where had they taken Ben? More to the point, where had they taken him *from*? Wherever the walls of the world had been punctured, a weakness would be left for up to three days. Other things—such as himself—might sneak through and back.

Lost between the bank and the pub. But he couldn't have been snatched from the car between those two places without causing chaos. He'd been pixie-led—guided inexorably to a spot of their choice and... The thought leapt up like an inspiration. They'd come through at Ben's house, seen him there first. His body would find it easy to take him there on autopilot while his mind was magic-mazed.

Very well. Try the house. Chris drove to Ben's work place and retraced the route he would have taken home, just to double check. No traffic jams, no upturned vehicles laced with claw marks. None of those goose-walking-over-one's-grave moments that Chris had learned to associate with a breakdown of the normal fibre of the world.

Ben's car was not in his drive. But could they have taken it while Ben dived out at the last moment and made a run for it? That too had got to be worth checking. Chris turned in and ruffled the immaculate gravel. The bell sounded shrill to him, the knocker portentous, but that was just nerves. He waited three minutes, knocked again and shouted while panic made blue lights fire up and down his spine, shrivelled his lungs in liquid nitrogen. "Ben? Are you in there?"

Pressing his ear to the glass brought sound, voices. It might not be too late after all! He tore around the back of the house, unclasped his pocket knife and cut through the plastic sheeting, sidled through into a blue-lit, cathedral-type space where the sitting room existed, half in, half outside. A liminal zone—they would like that, twilight creatures that they were.

The voices were louder here. The padlocked door stood between Chris and them, a man's voice and a woman's, raised in argument. He couldn't tell, with the muffled effect of the wood, if the man's voice was Ben's. "Ben? Is that you?"

They carried on as if they hadn't heard him while he looked around for something with which to force the door. The little black eye of a security camera gazed at him impassively as he returned from the garden with the pedestal of the birdbath under his arm. One blow of that, used as a battering ram to the padlock, and then another. The door boomed and splintered. The hasp of the lock stretched like rubber and snapped, and he ran inside still carrying the garden ornament, half-weapon, half-forgotten under his arm.

Empty rooms, freshly hoovered. He set the stone column down and brought out his knife again, turned the handle of the kitchen noiselessly. Edged it slowly, carefully open. A flood of sunlight glittering on spilled rain, tinted pink from the roses around the window. Countertops sparkled, and the Radio Four afternoon play spilled out remorselessly from a radio plugged into a timer on the wall. Security conscious Ben had set it to play in his absence, to fool the burglars into thinking he was at home.

Chris snapped it off, put the knife down on the countertop and staggered back to the table, sitting down while the battle readiness ebbed and left the shakes behind it.

Like amber and garnet in the sunlight, bottles of spirits lined one counter, cut-glass tumblers in a glass-fronted cabinet above. Chris took one down and half filled it, tossed it off and caught himself before he could repeat the performance. A bit of Dutch courage was good. Too much, less so. And there were still things he could do.

Sitting in the warm flood of sunshine, Chris took two deep breaths, counted to ten, and phoned Stan. The long drone of "number unobtainable" met his ear. He cursed his shaky hands, started again with slow care, making sure to get it right. But the result was the same. Cut off. That bloody father of his, no doubt. It was always the way—once one thing went wrong, it all went to hell together.

He left the tumbler in the sink, went out the way he'd come in, and within quarter of an hour was drawing up outside Stan's house. The family was in the front garden, having a barbecue—there was no need even to ring the bell before the shit hit the fan. All he had to do was to get out of the car.

He walked through the gate and onto the lawn as Stan's mum touched her husband on the arm and Fred put down the lemon he'd been drizzling on the chops and picked up the fire poker. Stan had been sitting in the shade of the porch, hunched over a handheld device, his gingery hair in his eyes and his white face more than usually sullen. He looked up as the bellow of his dad's shout broke the peace, and there was a kind of despairing gratitude in his eyes that Chris didn't feel he had time to deal with.

"Stan, they've got Ben. I need a trace on his phone. Can you do that?"

Chris dodged the flailing arms of Fred Grimshore, leapt back out of the way of the whistle of the poker.

"No problem, Mr. G, I'll just get my stuff." Stan was on his feet, dodging back into the house and closing the front door behind him. His mother gave a cry of distress or anger, dashed after him, but he had latched the door. She found keys, tried to turn them in the lock and found the door bolted on the inside. Distracted, Fred looked away, and Chris ran to the car, started it and got it round the back of the house just in time for Stan to drop first a rucksack and then himself out of his bedroom window onto the carefully positioned trampoline below, and thence onto the lawn. The boy vaulted over the low backyard fence, wrenched open the passenger door and poured himself inside.

Chris drove away as though there were five Junkers 88s on his tail.

"Fucking hell," said Stan, appreciatively, "that was like something out of the movies. Jailbreak! Are the cops on our tail and everything?"

"If they weren't before, they undoubtedly are now."

At Chris's expression, Stan's smile faltered. "They don't mean anything, my folks. Couple of windbags. Never done anything for me—tuition, parts, special skills—they didn't want none of it. They'd be happy if I went down the mill for the rest of my life. Philistines."

"Ben's phone?" Chris asked, and then moved by the softly stubborn expression, "Maybe they just didn't have the money for that stuff? Have you thought about the RAF? They'd sponsor you through college. For your mind, they'd think it was a bargain."

"Don't want to kill people, all due respect." Stan had extracted a black box from his bag, was now unfolding a spindly wire dish that looked as if it was made of kitchen sieves and coat hangers. Some sort of radar, Chris assumed, trying not to feel rebuked.

"Well, it feels different when the other fellow is also trying to kill you," he said, and took them out to the ring road where they could circle until they got a fix.

It came within minutes of Stan switching his contraption on. "Kind of left and a bit down," he said, pushing back his hood to see the readout clearer. "Out of town, up towards the hills." He waved his arm in an arc that made suspicion trickle like ice water down Chris's back.

Under the Hill: Dogfighters

Chris turned the car and began heading for the Nine Ladies stone circle, Stan confirming the turns all the way. The shapes of clouds and sunshine moved over the silver-grey road between its dry stone walls, gilded and silvered the green grass and the speedwell flowers, orange poppies and heather dark as yew. The bones of the country began to show beneath the skin.

"You know where you're going," said Stan, as Chris turned before the boy had a chance to tell him to.

Chris gave a gallows smile. "I'm guessing, but it's looking more likely with every turn. I hope... But, yes. Well..."

They had to draw up by the side of the road, and there was a layby and a little footpath, marked by ramblers, defaced by tossed-aside Coke cans and crisp packets. Stan squinted at the glare of the high sun as he got out—he was without his normal baseball cap. Chris fetched his fedora from the boot, landed it on top of Stan's head, making the boy smile. "It'll be okay, Mr. G, there's a good signal from his phone. He's probably asleep, right? Like Rip Van Winkle in the middle of the fairy ring. We'll wake him up and it'll be fine."

He angled the dish with hands that were heavily freckled by the sun. He had the overlarge hands and feet of a growing boy, and his voice slipped from girlish to growl midsentence. He was, Chris realised, very young. Perhaps too young to bring into this business. Though, God knew, Ashby Cunningham on B flight had been almost the same when he was shot down over Hamburg, having lied about his age on admissions.

There was no sign of the fog Ben had spoken of, though the wind was silky with moisture. Chris found a gap in the hedge, brushed past, taking cobwebs with him, scrambled up onto the field in which the nine stones stood. The dancers, they were called, witches, dancing at their sabbat out here in the lonely country under the swollen sky, who had been turned to stone by a passing saint with no regard for their families or friends.

It was a desolate sort of place, even in the searchlight glare of a strong sun. The great silence engulfed the small peeps of heather-dwelling moorland birds and the hiss of the wind. When a car went by on the distant road, all it did was to bring home the emptiness of the land before and after.

Nine dancers, apparently. One had fallen onto its side and was covered in moss and yellow lichen. A red mark on it looked like a handprint. It wasn't until one of the fingers began to elongate, to pool and drip that Chris realised it *was* a handprint—the print of a man's palm in blood.

Stan had seen it now, was frowning as though the sight did not compute. He looked up into Chris's face, down at the machine, fiddling with the dials unnecessarily. "Do you want to go back to the car?" Chris asked, seeing scraped-up turf, the gouged marks of a struggle. "I think I can find it from here."

Stan put his machine down with enormous care, then grabbed hold of Chris's pocket. "No way I'm going back to the car on my own. You know what'll happen then. I'm sticking with you."

Too many late-night horror films flashed into Chris's memory. "Good point. All right, we'll keep together. Hold on tight."

They shuffled up to the trampled ground. The long scars of claw marks dragged from the closest stone through the centre of the circle and out again to the base of the low hill behind. Beneath the red handprint, the moss had been torn away from the stone in furrows. Easy to see where Ben had tried to hold on, been pulled away, scouring the skin off one of his hands in the process.

Drag marks along the heathery turf and buttercups spattered red. A little farther on, a shoe lay by the side of the spoor, upside down, the toe all but scuffed off. Below the hill, a sliver of silver upended in a flowering gorse bush proved to be Ben's phone, still on, Chris's number called up on the menu.

Ten accusing furrows like claw marks showed where someone had scrabbled against the ground. They slid up to the hill, disappeared into a tiny hole, a badger's set. Crumbled soil around the base of it, and long, verdant grass at the top. Chris couldn't see in more than a foot, but he knew that—even if he could—he would not have been able to see through to where they had taken Ben. It should have been a comfort to know that the handprints did not really culminate in that earthen grave, but it wasn't.

Unwanted, the memory of Ben's flashback recurred to him—his terror of the underground, his parents' death, his need for a therapist. And to go like this, dragged into crumbling earth, clawing for purchase every step of the way...

Chris picked up the phone, bent over it, seeing his own face reflected in the scuffed plastic surface. God, he looked every bit of his near ninety years, and so he should. Pathetic old man, who had promised to protect Ben and failed, who had promised never to leave Geoff behind and broken that promise with a thoroughness that staggered. "Damn them. Damn them and damn me too."

After a short period of heartbreak, he tipped the phone into his pocket, looked up and found Stan kneeling next to the abandoned tracer. The boy's straggly hair looked as if it were made from copper wires, as though he'd become some kind of cyborg in sympathy with his machines, but no machine would have worn such a softly forlorn expression. "I thought this was going to be fun. Something to boast about to me mates at school..."

"It's all fun and games until somebody loses a war." With an effort, Chris smiled and helped the boy up. He gave a small snort of amusement—not because he felt it but because Stan looked in need of it, and he'd long ago had practice in faking it to cheer his crew. "Don't fret, lad. Look, he was still fighting when they took him. Chances are he's still alive. What we need is a way of opening this gateway again, and we need to do it in the next three days because the borders of the world have been weakened by this transfer."

He picked up the hat which had fallen at Stan's feet when he put the tracer down, dropped it once more over the small ginger head. "And I'm relying on you to find a way to do that. You're my secret weapon in this battle, lad. What can you give me?"

Chris began leading the boy away from the stones, hand on his shoulder to stop him from twisting around to look back. "I dunno, Mr. G," Stan said, cuddling the satellite dish of his tracer as if for comfort. "Open an interdimensional rift? Sounds kind of high-energy to me. Where are we going to get the power?"

"Reopening it," Chris said, breezily. He ushered Stan into the car, turned up the heater. What they both needed was a cup of tea, something sugary to counteract the shock. His house, then. "And I don't think it would need to be open for long. Grace was explaining something to me. If you could give me just a moment's help, just a turbocharge, I can do the rest."

The drive home passed in silence. Stan had taken out a school notebook and was drawing in it, his foxy brows knotted. He'd put his glasses on and the lenses were fogged up with moisture. Chris thought about offering a handkerchief, but in the end decided that it was kinder not to notice the tears at all.

There seemed to be some kind of incident going on next door, he thought as he turned into Snitterton Close and saw the police car parked in his neighbour's front drive. The lights were on, flashing blue over the hard faces of two uniformed police officers. When he turned into his drive, a third man behind the wheel of the car drove in behind him, blocking his escape.

He switched the engine off, put his head into his hands and pressed his thumbs to the bridge of his nose to forestall the incipient headache. A callused hand tapped at the driver's window. "Get out of the car, please."

"What...?" Stan raised his head, took off his glasses and wiped them. His face beneath was wet with tears.

"I'll, um...deal with this." Chris put his elbow down on the door lock for just enough time to say, "You get working on that portal problem, all right? Take it to Phyllis when you're done."

"Not you?"

"Huh. I think, um. I think we'll let your father calm down a little first. Okay? Anything you give to Phil will get to me in the end."

A hiss of intaken breath and Stan looked up as though he'd been slapped. He glowered at the policeman, who was now shaking the car by the door handle. "Is this my dad's fault? Did he set 'em on you?"

When Chris unlocked the doors, they were wrenched open immediately, and a large hand in a blue serge sleeve reached through and took him by one arm and the back of the collar in a professional sort of way. "Well, he's a man of his word," Chris said, trying to keep up the smile for the boy's sake. It was getting so hard to do that his face positively hurt with the effort.

"Fucking wanker!" Stan exploded with all the violence his asthmatic frame contained. "He's got no right to set the pigs on my friends just 'cause I'm actually learning something. You hear that, lady?"

A brisk, blonde policewoman with feathered hair and arctic eyes had emerged from the squad car to take care of the child. She bent down with a reassuring smile that didn't touch her cool, assessing gaze. "And who might you be, son?"

Her partner was grizzed, bald and fat, playing with the handcuffs on his belt meaningfully. "Are you Christopher John Gatrell of number two, Snitterton Close?"

Well, this was going to hell in a handbasket. "I am."

Still, he'd committed no crime, Stan would back him up. Trip down to the station, evening of unpleasantness, it would give the boy time to think of something. Then he could hop in the car, drive to Langdale, borrow his "sacrament" and make an assault on the realm of Faerie. He guessed he could give them an evening when he'd only otherwise be spending it in misery and self-reproach.

"I'm going to have to ask you to accompany me down to the station."

"Of course. May I ask what I'm accused of?"

"Most innocent people don't assume they're accused of anything."

"Most innocent people haven't just had a run-in with the boy's father," Chris said. "Unpleasant man. Seems to regard giving the boy an after-school job as some kind of perversion."

"Is that right?" The policeman wrote down *some kind of perversion* in his notebook. His face compressed together, as though someone were squeezing the juice out. "As a matter of fact we have evidence linking you with a break-in at 20 Castle Road, Bakewell. The owner of which property seems to have gone missing in mysterious circumstances. But we'll take the matter of the boy under review too, if you like."

Opening the door of the squad car, he folded Chris into it, Chris unresisting, feeling like he were freefalling—like he'd just pulled the parachute cord and seen the canopy unravel, snap and blow away. "A break-in?"

"That's right. I should caution you that you do not have to say anything. But it may harm your defence if you do not mention when questioned something which you later rely on in court. Anything you do say may be given in evidence."

Too late to struggle now, Chris thought as the officer got in the back with him and the car began to drive away, leaving the policewoman and Stan behind, the boy looking confused and very small. *But fuck.* There really wasn't any better word for it. *Just fuck.*

Chapter Three

The minute the grip let go of his ankle, Ben was up and fighting, a stone for a club in his hand, and in his head the raw madness and terror of the bomb. He hardly saw the shapes ranged about him as he staggered out of the earth and onto marshy wet ground. He was struggling with the falling walls, the shrieking train, tapping into the berserker strength of a man fighting for his mother, for his father's life.

He cut them down like a scythe through grass and ran, trying to get out, get out, and back to his car...get back to...

Brightness began to filter through his awareness—a pearl-grey sky above, the sound of water. Then his ankle was grabbed again and pulled out from under him, and time disjointed again under the impact of his panic. The ground blurred beneath him as he was picked up and carried, upside down, into the sky. Below him, a river twisted. Above him, he could finally see the thing that had brought him here. From its black snout to the lashing black coils of its tail, it was full forty feet long and had the lazy smirk of a crocodile.

"No!" He twisted up, not sure if this was real or if he was still in the grip of madness, and hammered his stone against the beds of its claws, making the dragon jerk and the meadow beneath him swing in dizzying circles. God, they were going fast now, a line of trees rushed towards him and a moment later all he could see was forest below. Some thoughts began to come back online—chief among them the expectation that the forest would sweep up to a mountain, and in that mountain would be the creature's lair, where he would end his life in its larder.

"No!" he shouted again. "Fuck you. No, I am not... Let me go!"

He got in a better hit, wedging the stone deep in the softer skin between its smallest digit and the next, heard the yowl of protest and had time to think *Oh shit!* before he was falling headfirst straight down towards the trees.

Branches broke his fall, just. The canopy was tangled, resilient. He grabbed for it, managed to get himself turned around, slid, breaking branches and maybe bones from one perch to the next, tearing further his crimson hands, and not feeling any of it as it rushed towards him and past.

Then he was on the ground and shaking, and the blur inside his mind resolved into the pattern of twigs on leaf mould all around him, the smell of soil and sap, and a gap in the star cover above him through which came a green light and the shadow of circling dragon wings.

The pain didn't come until he had got up, seen a suggestion of light ahead of him and begun to thread his way through the silent trees towards it, but it had been like this during the bombing of the underground too superhuman strength, a numbness to pain, and when it wore off, a mental wound that still hadn't completely scabbed over.

Yeah, don't think of that. Just get somewhere safe. Okay? Just get... He stumbled over something, was bemused to see it was a helmet, lying between the tree roots, quite clean and unrusted. They were all over the place, in fact, coats of mail lying folded on top of quilted padding, surcoats, green and grey as the wood around him. They lay as if ready for an inspection, bowed and whispered over by the trees. Then a darkness moved in the corner of his eye—he glanced towards it, saw only spiders, scuttling into the cracks of the tree trunks—and when he looked back, the armour was stones and piles of leaves, and he wondered if he'd ever seen it at all.

A thin, high screech came, maybe nothing more than a branch rubbing against another branch, making a sound like nails on a blackboard, but it lanced straight through his head, pressed the button marked "panic", and he set his head down and ran as he had never run before. There was an odd pleasure to it, scrambling over roots, lunging from one patch of sunshine to the next, discovering to his surprise that he was surer footed, faster, stronger than he would have believed.

Was there something in the air? Was the gravity lower? He felt as though he could run forever, as though it was the only thing he needed to do. But then the tree cover began to draw away. He saw, ahead of him, a long slope up from forest to…to…

He would have stopped and gazed—meadow giving way to silver streets that curved about a massive artificial hill, round and regular as a bowl. Towers covered it—grey and more shades of grey, topped off with silver, hot and molten bright where sunlight beat against windows. A city.

He would have stopped and gazed, but when he looked up, he saw the reflection of the dragon move over the many towers, pushing through the air as inexorably, as perfectly as a Viking longship up an undefended estuary.

Couldn't stay among the trees, couldn't stand here on the meadow to be crisped. He got his breath back, summoned a now slightly watery strength, and dashed for the road.

The dragon was circling like a great vulture, head arched down towards the forest. He thought he could get to cover before it looked his way, was sure of it, breath hissing hot through his own teeth, and his legs burning under him. There was a bridge and an arch, if he could only get under...

And a moat opened up practically beneath his feet—a citywide defensive ditch, narrow but deep. Invisible until you were all but on top of it. He plunged in, jarred his already aching head, tumbled into a nest of brambles at the base of it and used every swear word in his vocabulary twice in a flood of profanity that would have purged him of everything, left him calm and collected, if it hadn't been for the dragon.

He lay still among the thorns and watched it circle against the empty sky. Around and around it went. So it hadn't seen him come out of the woods. It didn't know where he was.

The wave of relief that went over him was the worst thing that had happened since the claws. It told him he was safe and, in response, all his hurts rose up to overwhelm him at once. His head. *God.* His hands, his arms—scraped raw from elbow to fingertips. *Oh fuck.* His legs, cramping up after the long run, seizing solid.

His foot slipped into the ankle-deep mud at the bottom of the ditch. It was cold in the eternal shade. He thought it had darkened suddenly, but it was only his eyes blurring from fatigue and injury. It was all too easy to imagine himself falling face-down into the wet—drowning in a soup of algae and city waste. Not the way he would have preferred to go. Looking up again, he found the dragon had ridden higher in the thermal above the city, was nothing but a black dot that slowly faded out of sight against a sky of fumes.

It was gone. It wouldn't see him any more if he found himself a safer place to collapse.

With his last reserves of strength, Ben got hands and feet into the rough-laid stones of the ditch on its inner side and slowly pulled himself out, rolling over the lip and down into a square by the city's outer limits. There he sprawled, dry and dusty, with mazy sunshine soothing the road map of his bruises, and for a blessed moment he gave himself over to dark and velvety rest.

It lasted all too short a time before his head woke him by splitting apart. He could feel the gape, going all around his skull, through one eye and back around his jaw. The brain must be spilling out even now and sizzling on the strange grey metal of the pavement. *God, that hurts.* He pushed himself up onto an elbow—even that was sore—and squinted at the dazzle. At the movement, the headache gave the sort of throb that stole his breath, made his body heave and gag, but his mind had cleared enough to wonder, with the desolation of a lost child, what happened next. Where was he supposed to go to find help? What did they want from him?

He levered himself up to a kneeling position, everything swirling around him, full of sparks and colours. He could almost feel the air moving on his skin, smell a thousand different savours—metal and grease, dust, heat and coriander, kerosine and smog. Not quite what he'd expected from Faerieland.

Nor, to be frank, were the skyscrapers—every shade of metallic grey from pewter to platinum. Carved in a riot of invention, strung together with walkways as delicate as cobweb, painted with shifting colours, they reflected the grimy light down onto streets lined with dying trees. Brown, crisped ivy and trailing plants wound up the mirrored surfaces and shed their leaves with every movement of the wind. Flakes of colour blew off and joined the thick dust on the ground. The corners of many of the buildings were scored and crumpled as if by clutching hands.

In the streets, bustle and energy and dilapidation went on unperturbed by his presence. Music in the distance, a voice calling out a single phrase again and again in a language he could not understand. Yellow lamps creaked above folk of many sorts, hurrying past with their heads down and the air of preoccupied misery he associated with London in the rush hour. Why hadn't they noticed him? Stopped what they were doing to stare at this invader of their world?

Only then did Ben notice that he was lying among other refuse, empty boxes, twisted metal and creatures, asleep, huddled into foetal balls, rocking. They were all—he too—covered in the dust, grey as the road. That figure over by the wall of the dried-up fountain, he surely must be dead, with half his head and torso missing like that.

The severed man opened his one remaining eye, looked at Ben without curiosity, closed it again. At this angle, Ben could see the veins pulsing in his open throat. He scrambled to his feet, and as he did so, a change came over the quality of the light—a dark, sweeping shadow ran along the distant boulevard, turning silver pedestrians, silver floating cars the colour of pared lead. Ben looked up as the shade passed over him and a wave of cold made his skin ripple.

The courtyard in which he'd lain boiled with activity as his fellow dossers scrabbled to their feet, ran for cover.

Darkness in the shape of spread reptilian wings passed over him, made a fluid black spiral in the air and came rushing back towards him like a hurricane.

Teeth. Teeth that looked like crystal daggers. Something lapping around its jaws and nostrils—a fume of smoke and the little flickers of violet flame. Shit! It had found him again.

Ben turned on his heel and ran. Up towards what might have been shops, crystals and spilled fruit skidding and mashing beneath his feet. Above him, windows slammed closed. He heard footsteps, running away, tried doors, but they had no handles, all he did was to make his fingers bleed again scrabbling at the cracks.

Far up the street, steps went down into darkness. If this had been London, he would have said it was an entrance to the underground tube stations. Here, who knew? Maybe the skyscrapers were only half of it, and the city went as deep down under the earth. At any rate, it was the entrance to a tunnel through which the dragon was too huge to pass. Part of Ben told him, *Cover. Run for cover.* A stronger part cowered, more afraid of reliving the nightmares down there than it was of the oncoming storm.

The dragon flapped its huge wings with a sound like the crack of a bullwhip. Ben ran for the tunnel, but it felt like running through treacle, running in a nightmare when one cannot move no matter how hard one tries. He made it to the first downward step and there his limbs refused his will, left him shuddering all over, unable to go any farther, with little pulses of memory throbbing in his mind, presaging a full-scale flashback. *Not now. For God's sake, not now.*

The dragon landed with a rush and a run, its long claws gouging holes in the silver surface of the road, its tail displacing parked vehicles, knocking down the tall, ornately carved lanterns that lined the road, dragging them behind it by the wires, a chain of lights chrysanthemum gold. The pulsing rumble of its breath sounded like laughter.

It paced slowly closer. He could hear it breathe in, the huge forge-bellows of its lungs inflating with a sound like the tide coming in. Ben took one more step down, but the memory of being pulled under the earth was too fresh and he could not make himself go any farther. In desperation, he stooped to pick up a stone, threw. It bounced off the slickly scaled snout. Fire flickered in the creature's nostrils and behind the uncomfortably sentient eyes. "Fuck!"

A sound broke through the battering of his heart. Hoofbeats. The dragon heard it too—it lifted its long neck and looked.

From the crossroads, out of the haze of gleaming dust and smog, a white shape tore, like clouds, like feathers, like the wings of angels. It came into focus, dazzling like snow under sunshine—a knight on horseback, in armour of silver, with streaming hair of silver-steel. With no time for cynicism, Ben felt a lift of the heart that was pure fairytale at the sight, as though the image had short-circuited a lifetime's wariness. It didn't occur to him not to reach up and take the hand offered to him, nor to feel comprehensively rescued.

He leapt up as the knight pulled, landed gracelessly half on the back of the swan-white creature that was his rescuer's mount. "Hold on to me," said a voice he recognised with a thousand stinging thrills, and the horse's wings snapped out, beat twice, and they were in the air.

The dragon stood on its tail and breathed out a raging blue inferno of flame that singed the horse's tail and the fetlocks of its legs. The horse gave a shrill, birdlike whinny and leapt forward. Behind them, Ben could see the dragon pacing across the street, climbing laboriously up the side of one of the buildings—a network of scores and creases in the mirror finish said it had done so many times before—trying to gain height enough to launch out and become airborne once more. But before it could do so, the mist closed behind them, and Ben was alone with his white knight in a sphere of pearl light and feathers and a rushing wind.

"Erm... Thank you," he said, breathing hard, this second burst of adrenaline draining faster than the first, leaving his hands shaking, his muscles stretched to the point of tearing, even his hair heavy. The wind against his skin was frigid, and something pricked at his eyes. He loosened a hand from the knight's slim waist and felt his eyelids—they were crusted with ice.

"Thank you for saving me, but we're too—we're too far up." Panic came back in a wave. The air scalded him with cold as he breathed it in, but he couldn't get enough of it to fill his lungs. The blinding, shrill pain of his head returned as if every brain cell was made of broken glass, and when he looked up he could see that the white sky had become indigo. The world was very far beneath him, and still they climbed. "We're too far up. I can't breathe!"

Why had he assumed this was a rescue? Why had he trusted anything in this place? What did he do now?

He tried to shake the knight, make him listen. "I can't..." he gasped. Things were fracturing, falling away, he felt his skin pull off with a feeling of relief. Sleep came, numb at first, comforting after.

He woke up in a palace.

Red coverlets swaddled him, warm and soft as fur, but interwoven with gold threads that stirred and glittered with every movement. When he sat, he found he had been dressed in clothes of the same material, white trousers, white shirt and a sash of cloth of gold. Reaching up, he examined his head and face with his fingertips, then turned his palms over with surprise. They had been scraped raw, oozing blood. Now they were whole again. He shoved up his sleeves, and his arms moved without pain, despite the wrenching they had had falling through tree branches. Even the muscular aches of unaccustomed frantic flight were gone.

Trying to sit up in this pool of lapping red material was harder than it seemed. It was slippery as ice, softly entangling. He wasn't sure he had the energy to fight his way all the way out. So tired, and so warm.

The roof above him was lapis lazuli blue, shot like the stone full of glints of gold. Three doors led off the round room in which he lay. They were all closed, but sounds of movement came from behind the emerald-painted archway of the nearest, where a vine scroll, painted onto the wood, seemed to move and slowly unwind as he watched.

It flowered, the door dissolving beneath it, and his rescuer walked through. Out of his armour, he wore a long tunic of dark blue velvet and carried a chalice—still looked like something stepped from a pre-Raphaelite painting. Ben recognised the face at once, though he'd only half-seen it before, outlined in bright strokes against a dim suburban night. There was no forgetting the hawklike beauty, or the hair like strands of platinum, cobweb fine, which rose and floated with his movement as though the air was buoyant as water to him.

"What happened?" Ben asked, the first and simplest of his many questions.

"I found you in a dangerous place and brought you away." The knight's narrow mouth was a pearly shade of pink, tilted up at the edges into a smile Ben felt bordered too nearly on the smug. "I had forgotten that you were human now and could not bear to go above the clouds unprotected. But no need to fret, we are safely home, as you see."

"Home?" Ben asked, and then, "Human *now*?"

"I have missed you so grievously, Karshni. And yet it pleases me immensely to think you did not take your father's part after all. You did not abandon me of your own will. It has been a great comfort to me to know that, though I own it shocks

67

me what he did to you. I never intended this, you must believe me."

They must have given him something to heal his wounds, and it had left him groggy, obsessed with the need to sleep to the exclusion of everything else. He tried to wrap his mind around what the creature was saying, abandoned the effort as too hard, and gazed at it without comprehension. It was very pleasant to look at, especially with the expression of hope and fondness and apology that was shading further towards worry the longer he watched.

"You do remember me?" His rescuer knelt by the bed, putting the cup carefully down on the floor beside him. He was perhaps seven feet tall, slender as a rush and nacreous as pearl. His skin had a sheen on it like the dew on a white grape, and his eyes were indigo and golden as the skyscape above Ben's head.

"We haven't exactly met."

At Ben's blank look, the creature brushed back its hair, tucked it behind a pointed ear. His smile saddened. "But we have, many times. I am Arran. We were something greater than friends, other than brothers."

"All I remember is you asking me which eye I saw you with." Ben tried to swallow, his mouth dry. Arran radiated a kind of static electricity, and the prickle of it beat on Ben's tongue and the inside of his mouth, making them feel swollen, achy. "I didn't know what you meant at the time, but I looked it up. If I'd have told you which one, you would have cut it out. Are you going to blind me now?"

He tried to get his feet under him, but they were buried under too many layers of the slithery bedclothes—he wondered if it was a bed at all and not a trap. Arran put out a long-fingered hand and set it gently on Ben's hair, rubbing the strands between his fingertips with a look of curiosity. Light flashed in little fireworks as he moved. His nails were covered in diamonds. "That was before I recognised you. I do not look closely at meat. A slight resemblance was not enough to jump to such an outré conclusion."

"You don't look at *meat*?"

"Humans." Arran laughed. "Look not so appalled. You have called them worse in your time." He picked up the goblet and offered it to Ben. When Ben made no move to take it, he lifted Ben's hand in his and wrapped the fingers around the stem. It was a tender gesture, and his voice was sorrowful when he concluded. "Truly, you remember nothing at all?"

"I remember nothing because there's nothing to remember." Ben tried to get angry. This was some kind of mind-fuck, softening him up for something. "I *am* human."

Another time there would be all kinds of depths of despair behind that cry, but it was hard to connect with them just now when the fear that had powered him for days had drained away and terror taken all his energy with it. Arran's touch was soothing, and the smell of the drink was like nutmeg and camphor, like *paan*. A smell from so long ago he never knew before how much it made him think of home.

He wondered if it tasted the same, brought it to his lips, Arran helping him to sit up, supporting him. The look on the creature's face now was kindly, warm as the bedclothes. A little scar on one cheek made Ben feel fondly towards him, though he couldn't quite place why.

"Sip," said Arran. "It's hot. To get the cold of the high places from your blood."

Cinnamon in Ben's mouth, and something creamy that coated his tongue and his throat and all his insides with slippery, prickly warmth. The room swam out of focus and the stars danced above him. A sane, priggish part of his personality told him, disapprovingly, that he had just been drugged, but he wasn't listening as he reached up to guide Arran's smiling mouth to his. Other than brothers, better than friends? Yes, why ever not?

The kiss was just as he'd imagined—like lightning pouring into him, but he was unravelling and becoming a cloud, and all it did was light him up, every last particle of him. Someone laughed. He thought it was himself, steeped in happy dreams, realised it was his lover just as the flesh under his fingertips became liquid as water and everything changed again.

Chapter Four

The police left Chris locked in the interview room for an hour, staring at blank institutional green walls, and a small square of window high up on the northern wall, against which rain slanted with a tick, tick, tick as if to emphasise the fact there was no other clock in the room. No doubt they intended to install a general terror, summon up guilt and nerves and destabilise him. It worked.

Chris picked at his cuffs, paced to the door and back, tried the handle at least fifteen times and tried not to mutter under his breath. A little black eye in the corner showed a red light, where the camera recorded his every movement. He tried to think back to what he'd been taught about resisting German interrogation, but those lessons seemed terribly long ago, in a remote and vanished world. How much time was passing in Faerie while he cooled his heels in here? How much longer would they be?

Long after he had abandoned hope, the door opened and two men came through. Not his policemen of earlier, these were higher-ups, plain-clothes. An older man so thin you could have used him for a scythe and a younger, already going slightly to fat, with a plump, pleasant face and a pair of girlish lips that undermined his stern expression. The younger man propped himself by the door, brought out a notepad. The older sat down across the table from Chris and steepled his hands like Mr. Spock from *Star Trek*.

"Mr. Gatrell?" He looked at his watch. "Interview begins at 22.21, Monday 17th of August." He smiled, rather like a cheese wire being drawn through a piece of Stilton. "We have to say that for the tape. All right then." When he nodded, his silent partner placed the bagged contents of Chris's pockets on the table and looked at him as though Chris should somehow be shocked.

"Are these your belongings, Mr. Gatrell?"

"The wallet and keys are mine. That one's my phone. That one..." Oh. As he looked at Ben's phone, covered in soil and blood, found in his pocket, a kind of creeping feeling came over him, like stepping in a pool and feeling, from the slow upwards drench of cold, that there's a hole in your shoe and the water's getting in. A chill rose up from his belly and touched his chest and throat. "That one is Ben's."

"That would be Mr. Ben Chaudhry of Castle Road, Bakewell?"

"Yes."

"Would you like to explain how you came to be carrying Mr. Chaudhry's phone? I should tell you that forensics are running a check on the blood as we speak. Yours, is it? Cut yourself shaving?"

Chris pressed the knuckle of his index finger to his lips to hold in the automatic rude retort. He tried to weigh up how much of the truth he could tell without appearing to be a dangerous madman. Very little, apparently. "I think you should tell me what I'm being accused of."

"I think you should stop wasting our time, Mr. Gatrell. Where did you get the phone?"

He'd played for time, thought of an answer now—the truth, as far as it went. "Ben phoned me up. He seemed very distressed—asking for help, saying someone was trying to abduct him." Chris folded his hands in his lap.

"He didn't tell me where he was. I presume there'll be records of the conversation stored on the phone? He was in a state and rang off before I could ask him. So I went to his house. I thought I could hear someone in there, but they weren't answering me. I was concerned for his safety, so I let myself in."

"Broke in."

"I would have had his permission, if I'd been able to ask. I thought he was being attacked. But yes. Broke in, if you like."

"We have that part on camera," commented the younger man, looking up from his notes. "Mr. Chaudhry was a security-conscious man, wasn't he? Never seen a bloke with CCTV in his house before."

"As I said, he was afraid there was someone out to get him. He installed the cameras quite recently, to protect himself, or to at least catch evidence."

"Which they seem to have succeeded in very well." The older man wore a nametag. DI Carter. His suit was shabby Marks and Sparks polyester, gone shiny at the cuffs. His eyes were blue but gave the impression of colourlessness, not giving anything away.

"You'll have seen me come in, find out that the noises I thought were conversation were in fact the radio, have a drink and go out again." The queasy sensation in Chris's stomach settled a little as he ran through his story and found it good.

"After that, I called at Stan's house. Stan Grimshore, that is. He's a technical wizz-kid—"

"Aged fifteen."

"Yes." Chris fixed the man with a firm gaze. "Yes, he's fifteen. He does some after-school work for me, building electronic devices. I thought he might have a way of tracing Ben's phone."

The door opened again, and a woman police constable came in, carrying a tray full of mugs of tea. There was one for him, and he drank it gratefully. Maybe he shouldn't have been braced for Gestapo-level unpleasantness after all. "And he did. We took the machine, got in the car and tracked Ben's phone down to the Nine Ladies. There'd been..."

The tea made a bid to come back up as he remembered the handprint, the tramlines of desperate claw marks in the soil, and the hole in the hillside. "There'd been a struggle of some kind. I found the phone under the hill, put it in my pocket without thinking. Then, because I didn't know what to do next, I drove home, and your people met me there."

"The Nine Ladies?" DI Carter nodded at his assistant. "Better get a team down there. See what you can find."

He waited for the door to close, the stale air to settle once more in a room as featureless as limbo, then he clasped his hands together again and leaned forward. "These...people...that Mr. Chaudhry was afraid of? Who were they?"

Dread welled up once more. Reassuring, surely, to think how quick the police were to come to the point. Or it would be, if he could answer. He weighed the possibility of a breaking-and-entry conviction against the certainty of Air Vice-Marshal Henderson's wrath, and said, "I couldn't say, sir. That information is classified."

Carter sipped his tea, his little finger held out in a genteel curve. Placing it carefully back in the saucer, he pulled a large brown file towards himself, flipped it open. Chris recognised his own picture, upside down, still in uniform, looking young and dazed and gormless.

"Says here," the inspector began, with another of his hair-thin smiles, "you run an outfit called Matlock Paranormal. Hunting down ghosties. You going to tell us Mr. Chaudhry was taken away in a UFO? Sucked down into the underworld by giant illuminati lizards?"

"I'm *not* going to tell you that. No, Inspector."

Carter turned back a few pages, put his forefinger gently down in the centre of a report on headed hospital notepaper. "Says here you were invalided out of the RAF on grounds of insanity. Now we've got a missing man. You were seen breaking into his house, his bloody phone is in your pocket, you give us a cock-and-bull story about classified information. I've got to say, Mr. Gatrell, things are not looking good for you. You'd better hope Mr. Chaudhry turns up soon, safe and well, or what we may be charging you with..." he paused, winched his smile tighter for dramatic effect, wiped his moustache and finished, "...is murder."

Murder? Murder meant no bail. Murder meant he'd be stuck in here for days while they gathered information, longer if they somehow managed to build a case. "Can you have murder without a body?"

Carter beamed and even his eyes flickered with colour for a moment. "Oh, interesting question. Again, not exactly what an innocent man would ask. So what have you done with it, then?"

And all that time, Ben could be in danger. A day in this world could be a hundred over there. He could be believing himself abandoned—as Geoff surely did—he could already be changed beyond all recognition. Lost.

"I have to get out of here. I can't be sidetracked by this. I don't have time..."

"You want to take your phone call now? I'm thinking you'll be needing a lawyer."

Outside the high windows, a platoon of fit young men were square-bashing, marching up and down, all with serious expressions and shiny shoes. Phyllis put her handbag down on the desk and sank into the chair offered. The man opposite looked young to her, but everyone did, these days. He certainly had enough gold braid on his sleeves to open a factory.

"Air Vice-Marshal Henderson?"

"Miss...?"

Huh. As if he didn't know. Phyllis primmed up her mouth, disappointed in him already. What was the point of looking so clean cut if you were only going to dirty it by playing silly buggers? "Mrs. Phyllis Mountjoy." She tapped on the desk, indicating the precise line of his report with her picture, name and address. "As you well know."

"What can I do for you, Mrs. Mountjoy?"

He was worried, she thought. Not a flicker of an emotion on that parade-ground face, but his collar was limp and there was a suggestion of damp around his temples. His buzz-cut hair looked dark with moisture. Sweating.

"I'm here to ask you to see to it that the police release Wing Commander Gatrell at once."

He crinkled his forehead at her, too artificially for it to really be called a frown. "I don't recall the name."

"Stop talking nonsense, young man." She pulled the manila folder out from under his hand, let him read the name on the label. "You know of him because I mentioned him. And if he had not been important, you would not have invited me here for this little chat. No point in being coy now."

The vice-marshal smiled. This expression she judged to be at least half-genuine, so she returned it with a slight upturn of her own lips. Nothing, she hoped, at all like triumph.

Out on the parade ground, the sound of shouting gave way to the rhythmic thud of marching and a lone voice calling, "Left, right. Left right left."

Henderson realigned his files and leaned forwards. "I will admit I was curious to see what Gatrell was up to these days. The Service feels a certain amount of paternal concern for those of its members who might be said to have been injured in the course of duty. Gatrell's breakdown... Very sad, of course. Not sure what you expect me to do about it."

"He is in jail."

"I'm aware—"

"Awaiting trial for a murder that he certainly didn't commit. That probably hasn't even happened yet."

"Yes. And again, I say to you, what business of mine is this? Unfortunate that his insanity has led to this, but really not my problem."

"I bet it isn't." Phyllis fished the photographs out of her bag, unfolded them and passed them over.

Phil, he'd said, over the phone from the police station, calling her in place of a lawyer. *In a suitcase under my bed. My insurance policy. Copy everything. One copy to Grace, one to yourself, and take another to Air Vice-Marshal Henderson. Tell him, prepare for an invasion. Tell him, I could help, if I was free. He could put pressure on, make them give me bail at least. I only need a couple of days to try to get Ben and Geoff back. And once Ben's back, this all collapses, you see?*

"These, however, are your problem," she said, placing them down in front of him one by one. Shocking things—a photograph of a wrecked plane, Chris and something else blackened, vaguely humanoid, in the burning debris. The body in the mortuary, the forensic reports, copies of letters, some with Henderson's signature attached. Shocking things—things she scarcely believed herself.

His face went rigid as rigour mortis again while he leafed through the stack. Pearls of sweat broke out on his forehead and rolled down his temples. "These are classified documents. Where did you get these?"

She felt a little sick, brought her handkerchief out of her bag and wiped her upper lip, the dab of lavender scent on the linen was calming. There were pink roses embroidered in one corner of the square—her mother's work. That too bolstered her courage, for her mother would have made short shrift of Henderson and his ilk. Soldiers, scarcely a step up from servants.

"The originals are in a safe place. Copies are with several members of our group, all of whom have been instructed to send them to the national press in the event of anything untoward happening to me today."

She'd thought that was paranoia, for the British government was not like these foreign despots who disappeared people all over the place, but she caught the movement of his left hand as he brought it out from under the desk, placed it flat on the surface. Had he been going for a button? A gun? Surely not.

"Definitive proof of time travel, flying saucers, hostile extraterrestrial life, and the fact that the RAF, in collusion with the government, hushed it all up. I'm sure you don't want the public to know about this."

He mopped his stubbly head with his own much larger hanky. Then he sighed. "We gave the man a new life. New identity papers, even a pension. What more does he want? It's not carte blanche to murder and get away with it. This is nothing more than blackmail."

"Don't be absurd." Phyllis was really getting rather cross with the man. What happened to taking responsibility? You expected this weaselly behaviour from politicians these days, but she'd hoped for better from the boys in blue. "I thought I'd explained it wasn't murder. These creatures that took him, all those years ago, have now taken another young man, and Chris is getting blamed for it. As a matter of fact he was trying to stop it."

"Nevertheless." The vice-marshal leaned back, looked out at the now-empty parade ground and the barbed-wire fence beyond. The base sat in acres of pine trees, screened from the world. *Far away from criticism*, Phyllis thought, and pulled the papers back towards herself.

"It would be quite convenient should Gatrell be put away for murder. Less chance of anyone believing anything he said. The whole thing could be dismissed as an imaginative attempt to cover up a sordid little murder. Good-looking young man, was he? The victim? Our boy Gatrell had a caution on record for being too ready to notice such things. One more mad, dead gay, eh? Who's going to argue with that?"

Phyllis grasped her handbag tight and pulled it against herself like Kevlar armour. For a moment she was completely lost for words. "You know, you have no idea why I'm here, and I have a mind to let it stay that way. I should like to see you caught on the hop and humiliated. If it wasn't that the nation, perhaps the world, was at risk, I'd leave now and let you take the flak."

Henderson rose, leaned forward, his spread hands braced on his desk and his face close to hers. She stiffened her upper lip, raised her chin and glared at him.

"What on earth are you talking about?"

"I was *sent* to give you a warning." Of its own accord, her right hand betrayed her state of mind by opening and closing her bag with a tap, tap of clasp like the sound of a stopwatch, counting down. "Chris believes that the abduction of Mr. Chaudhry is only the start. He's received warnings that there is to be an invasion. You should put your troops on...red alert or whatever it is."

"On the word of a madman?"

"You *know* he isn't mad. You're the one who gave the order to cover up all the evidence last time. You know what these things can do—at least, you know they can break time, shoot down a plane in the forties and have it land in the nineties. Aren't you at all concerned about the safety of your country?"

Henderson stalked stiffly to the door and opened it, stood in the arch, looking out. Somewhere along the white corridor came the sound of a whistle, booted feet and surprising, generous laughter. At the sound of it, the air vice-marshal relaxed. He passed his hanky over his hair. "Perhaps I am concerned. But you must admit, Gatrell's behaviour has been...eccentric since he left the service. He may not have been insane when he was discharged, but I don't know the state of his mind now."

He gave his wintery smile. "I don't know what hold he has over you. This must have been something of an ordeal for you. Why would you come here, put yourself through this, for him?"

"Because I'm a patriotic Englishwoman who believes it's her duty to do her bit for her country?"

"Hm. That may even be true. But why believe him in the first place? All of these things could be faked."

Phyllis looked again at the upside-down photograph with her name beneath it. Beneath that, her life story. "I lost my children—you've seen. After the accident I felt very useless for a long time. No one should outlive the purpose of their life. But he needed me. They all do. The MPA. But Chris especially. I thought at first it was just one of those things. Now I know it was because he lost his world too. We have all been trying to build something new and good to replace what was stolen from us. We have all been in the same boat."

"Sentiment." Henderson closed the door and leaned on it, but his face had softened.

Phyllis raised her eyebrows at him. "Or instinct. Besides, do you have no sentiment of your own? The man was a pathfinder in World War Two. Distinguished Flying Cross. A genuine war hero. One of the very few, and the only one who could still be under your command. That doesn't mean anything to you? You don't think he's owed a little trust?"

Henderson gave a soundless snort of amusement. "Well, since you put it that way. The man's not really loopy, I take it?"

"I would say not. You've seen some things, I'm sure. I've seen more. And Chris"—this was probably an unwise thing to say, but she was going to say it anyway—"he's been our squadron leader. We've trusted him and come out alive from situations I would not like to face alone. I think if there *is* some sort of alien invasion planned, the country would be better off with him out of jail and able to deal with it. And of course, you can always re-arrest him later. He's not the kind of man to do a runner, as they say on TV."

Henderson drifted back to his desk, sat down, mopped his brow and reached for the telephone. "Very well," he said, punching in a string of nine numbers and hesitating over the last. "I'll have a word with the chief of police. But we'll be watching carefully, you understand? I want that man of his to turn up alive within the month or I pull the plug on the whole thing and send him back."

"I'm sure," Phyllis pinched herself beneath the desk, just to choke back the exclamations and effusive thanks, "that you won't have any cause to regret this, sir. Thank you."

"Well, if all my visitors were as charming as you…"

When she was out of the door, she had to stop and check her reflection in her hand mirror. She hadn't suddenly lost ten years. Feather-cut silver hair and bright blue eyes, rose-petal pink lipstick aside, she still looked like the grandmother she would have been, had a cruel fate not intervened. She gazed a little longer and then laughed, going out through the gates with a spring in her step. Brylcreem boys! Some things clearly never changed.

Chris stood at parade rest in the DI's office, eyes forward, fixed on the Manchester United calendar. One glance at Carter's face had been enough. "Friends in high places, eh?" said the inspector. "Well, that doesn't carry any weight with us. We'll be watching you. You try to leave the country and we'll have you. And one more hint of anything illegal and we'll do you so hard you won't know your own name. Understand? Plenty of time to get the evidence to convict you, so don't think you're out of the woods yet."

"I can go?" The frantic thoughts of escape that had plagued him overnight—somehow cutting his way out of a police van en route to the magistrate's court, perhaps, or knocking out a prison guard, swapping clothes, blagging his way out at the guard's end of shift—fell away in a moment of profound relief. They wouldn't have worked anyway. They would just have made things worse. But he would have felt honour bound to try it regardless. Now, thank God, he didn't have to. He only had to somehow force entry into the world of Faerie, confront its queen and her invasion force, and snatch back two of her hostages. That seemed easy by comparison.

"Sergeant Devlin will take you to pick up your effects. You can go for now."

Thank you, God. Thank you, Phyllis—I knew you could do it. And thank you, Air Vice-Marshal Henderson. It looked like the brass hats did still care after all. Not like Butcher Harris of course—this soft and flabby modern world couldn't support a man like him any more. But they still knew how to throw a gamble, make the big gesture now and again.

The thought made him square his shoulders and want to salute. One more person not to let down. *Yes, sir!*

Chapter Five

Ben floated downwards towards reality like a seed on the wind. His mind was full of chariots and forests where he rode behind a charioteer in a turbaned helmet glorious with feathers, a parasol above him, its fringes aglitter with gold. He felt the pull of a great bow as the wind tugged at his long hair and the *dhoti* that he wore, blue and silver as the sky glimpsed amid the fluttering leaves.

Beside him, in a lighter, faster, one-man chariot, Arran sped, blood like a caste mark on his forehead and dripping down his snow-white arms, bespattering the golden torc around his neck. Other than jewellery and a twist of leather to hold back that floating silver hair, he wore nothing at all, and Ben's dream-self did not appear to think this unusual. He'd long ago got over being shocked by what the barbarian got up to.

Waking came so subtly that it was several long, relaxed heartbeats before he realised he had passed out of the dream and into reality. When he did, it was with a sensation like double vision. He remembered this place—remembered Arran's chambers with old familiarity. And he also remembered never having been here before last night, when he was kidnapped and drugged.

Some pretty powerful stuff. He wondered if the memory of disturbing, changeable sex was dream or reality. It had a dreamlike texture, but so did everything here. Despite his boast to Chris that he was entirely without hang-ups where sex was concerned, the thought that it could have been real made him feel queasy and unclean. He drew the line at interspecies date rape.

Crawling out of the bed with some difficulty (this morning it was blue, like a little pond of silk) he rolled out onto the marble floor, stood up and went looking for a bathroom. It lay behind the door he'd expected—a great cistern of cool water with steps down into it and a floor that threw back the light like black diamond. He remembered this too. Remembered that the flowers that floated there, when crushed, released a slippery, jasmine-scented sap that cleaned the body and left the hair glossy as polished jet.

Somehow the bath was not as calming as he would have liked. The double vision only compounded his queasiness. He was afraid to look too closely at the mirrored floor in case the wrong reflection looked back.

Climbing out, he found a wardrobe exactly where he expected it to be. Inside hung a number of outfits, long tunics and baggy trousers of exquisite cloth, that he felt he had a right to. He chose a suit of silk, the blue-green of a peacock's throat—interwoven with scenes of battle in gold thread. The buttons that held the neckline closed were carved out of huge single sapphires, and a chain of emeralds had been folded up atop it, swung to his waist when he put it over his head.

When he looked at himself in the still surface of the bathing pool, it was again with that feeling of vertigo. Ben thought, *I look like something from bloody Bollywood*, and someone else thought, *It is a little plain, but it will do.*

He sat down on the diamond floor. The water, flowing constantly into and out of the pool, made a sound like rain. The

85

flowers in the pool turned, one by one, from the white stars of jasmine to the ragged pink and gold of honeysuckle, and their new scent made the room cloying sweet. *Who the fuck are you?* Ben said to himself and felt a dim, far-off jolt of outrage that a Dalit had dared talk to *him* like that.

They were messing with his head, and—as Chris would say—they were doing a damn fine job of it. Going out once more into the main room, he tried the door, both expecting and not expecting it to be locked. It melted at his touch, like thawing snow, and let him out into the opalescent quiet of the nobles' quarter.

Under the trees at the centre of the square, a dreamweaver, a bard and a courtesan played a game of illusion, creating glittering dragons the size of Ben's hands, letting them spiral up, flying, fighting, giving tiny bursts of multicoloured flame as they fought to reach the arching ceiling. The air was full of them, glittery as toffee paper. They burst like bubbles when he tried to touch them, and the competitors crossed their hands on their breasts and cast down their eyes, standing statuelike and abased as he passed.

Okay. So they think I'm someone important. So I think I'm someone important. I can use that.

Ben considered saying, "Take me to your leader," the prick of hysteria never too far away. God, what he wouldn't give to wake up in the next half hour in hospital and find all of this had been just a dream.

The other part of him, proud and certain of himself—the part that he felt he should have known was there all along—rolled imaginary eyes at his obtuseness. *We will go to the palace*, it said. *The queen will have an explanation for what has happened. How you became embedded in my mind like a canker.*

No, it was official, he didn't like his other self a bit. But he let it guide him up the curved street, commandeer a horse from a lesser noble, order anyone who didn't look away fast enough to accompany him. A prince could not arrive alone—he must have a retinue.

There were musicians in his train and jugglers, a couple of young women who strewed the street with flowers, fourteen ill-at-ease guardsmen and a cooper with his tools as he arrived at the palace doors and found them open. There his expectations were soothed as courtiers bowed to the ground before him, laying down their silken cloaks in a path before the feet of his horse. He was assisted from his stolen horse by nymphs, had it led away to be stabled, while beautiful young men pressed drinks upon him and brought him to a throne one step down from the great pearl chair in which Queen Oonagh sat.

"My friend!" she said, leaping up and descending to his level, curling up by his feet on the step where his throne sat. "The servants will be whipped for not telling me you were recovered. I would not have had you arrive thus in meanness, had I known you willed to come here this day."

Ben put his foot down firmly on the part of his mind that was slightly mollified by this speech. "I don't know you," he said. "And you had no right to bring me here against my will."

She was a beautiful woman, all silver, with a look about the face that reminded him of Arran. He wondered if they were related, cousins perhaps. He seemed to remember reading somewhere that the old-fashioned royal dynasties were all horribly inbred.

Now she bowed her head, looking sad and fragile. "I am sorry you don't remember me, but I mean to help you remember. What looks to you at present as an abduction is a rescue, I assure you. Once you have recalled who you are, you will not wish to return to your exile."

"I have no idea what you're talking about," he said, and there came like an echo from a deep cave, muffled by distance, his other self's feeling of anguish and anger, betrayal and guilt.

"I only hope that your father's actions were not caused in part by our friendship. When you disappeared, we grieved, but we could not discover the truth. Your father"—she gave a small, sad laugh—"is not speaking to us at present, and he has closed the borders of his realm to us. We could not search for you against his will."

Uncurling, like a flower opening to the sun, she shook a head crowned with moonstones and offered him a hand. "But this is not a subject of which we should speak in public. Come, I have something I wish to show you. It may remind you, I hope, of who you are."

She led him to a stone door behind the dais. He crooked an elbow for her so she could lay her hand on his arm as they ascended, and she gave him a sideways glance full of pleasure and cunning that he recognised to the soles of his feet. No doubt about it, she was speaking at least some part of the truth—otherwise how could his other self be nodding along, going, *Yes. Yes, I remember. The privy chambers are to the left and down. I remember that she has another city of her own beneath the common levels. Little passages of hewn rock and chambers empty of everything but darkness. Temples with statues of forgotten gods.*

You trust her? he asked himself, and got back something complex. He trusted Arran, but he knew that Arran reported to the queen, that his loyalties were absolute, far more to be relied on than any words he spoke. It seemed Ben's other half admired this, and it grieved him that the same thing could not be said of himself.

He paced beside the queen, and his hand on her flesh seemed too heavy, as though he might break her accidentally. "Whoever you remember," he said, "that's not me. I am Ben Chaudhry of Bakewell in Derbyshire. I am a human being and I have my own life that I would like to go back to."

He thought about Chris, and the expected resentment didn't come. The man couldn't—not really—have been expected to be on guard at all times, to have hovered over Ben every hour of every day for the rest of his life. They'd got off to a bad start and carried on via one disaster after another, but Chris was what he thought about when he thought of home. The chance to pick up with him and argue their way into some kind of new life. Something real—to build something whole and wholesome out of their own shared emptinesses.

But Chris hated the fae with a passion. If Ben managed to find a way out, would he have to own up to being not entirely human himself? Would the passenger now riding in his head go away? Or was this all fucked up already, no way home?

"Here," said Oonagh, pushing open a huge round door into a room round as a bubble. In the centre of it was what looked like a beautiful sculpture of flowering vines, until Ben noticed that the thick, twisted metal rods of its construction were buried in the stone floor, the graceful curve of the wires disguised a brutal strength. Then he looked again and saw it was a cage.

In the cage two people floated, their utter stillness like that of the dead, unbreathing. He recognised them both with a clench of the heart that felt like being pulled inside out through the lungs.

"Your sister."

She was clad in the garments in which she would dance in the temple. He looked at her face and saw her dimly, the memories swimming up from somewhere deeper than his bones, tickling the back of his mind, bemusing him. "I don't have a sister."

Yes, it is she.

Looking at the man turned up the volume on his protests fiftyfold. God, yes, you didn't forget the face of a man who'd tried to kill you. But he was so...so real, in his dirty RAF fatigues, blood and mud on his face, weight and flesh and presence, he was so *human*. And Ben choked on that future he'd just been imagining, found it tasted exactly like the snot running down the back of his throat from unshed tears.

"And this man tried to kill me." He sniffed, but the words still came out thick, full of unpacked anguish. "What the hell's going on?"

She looked sharply interested. "He did, did he?" and circled the cage, looking in. "I have suspected that one of my political rivals has been telling him lies about me. It seems they have been telling him lies about you too. You do know that he could not have touched your world without powerful magic?"

"Well duh." Ben tried to lay his hands on the bars of the cage. There was a resistance there—he pressed and pressed but his hand moved no farther.

"Time is suspended inside the bubble," Oonagh said, watching him. "They were stored down with the other sleepers, but I had them brought up here so that you could examine them in more comfort." She picked up a rod of ivory that lay in a hollow beside the room's single slab-like seat and handed it to him. "This activates and deactivates the time field. In case you wish to free your sister. It wasn't my desire to keep her so strictly confined, but the two of them had begun to prove troublesome together. I could not allow that."

Ben took the wand and slumped into the chair, pinched the inside of his wrist and *ow*, that bloody hurt. "Imagine I don't remember anything." He looked again at the sleeping face of Geoff Baxendale and wondered how anyone's life could possibly be so screwed. "Who are you, what do you want with me? Start at the beginning and tell me all of it. Make me understand."

She laughed and touched the prison, making the polished pendant leaves tremble. The ghostly, sourceless light of the room flickered and pulsed like the meniscus of a stream, flashing off the ornaments of the cage. The cage rustled like a wood in a breeze, but the sleepers within did not move.

"I am Oonagh, queen of the Sidhe and of the Ylfe. And though you say 'the beginning', I think you will not wish me to tell you of the wars between those two. Suffice it to say, as the Saxons were to England, so the Ylfe were to Faerie. Long years since, and though we have become one people, that wound still aches betimes.

"This is old grief, but old grief does not fade for a people who are doomed to live for millions of years. So my land still harbours those who resent me and my decisions. It is made worse by the fact that I—and my mothers before me—have espoused progress, industry, invention. The discoveries we've made!"

Her smile was wry, her mouth all the more like Arran's with the twist of sarcasm on it. "But our progress has come at a great cost. Our land is dying. I walk among my people in disguise that I may know their true thoughts, and I see them sickening in the reek of it. Year by year I watch more of them fall to despair, and I see no way to save us if we may not depart and leave the land to heal.

"We have built ships, but they cannot be launched from this world—there is no longer the strength here to fuel them. You, Karshni, suggested that we launch them from your world. You were engaged on persuading your father. But then you disappeared and he would no longer speak to us, and the walls of your world were raised. Then we were desperate enough to capture your sister in order to force him to acknowledge us. But he has not done so, and time is running out."

"So what's your next step?" Ben asked, getting up and walking around the cage. Eerie, how they didn't move at all. They had a plastic look about them, like Lenin's mummy, displayed for the faithful in Moscow.

Oonagh laughed. "I found you again. My next step is to bring you here and ask for your help. We have been friends a long time, and this was always as much your plan as mine."

The other set of reactions, the other personality who rode along like a tattoo in the inner layers of his skin told him that she spoke the truth—that he had been here often, that he had chosen Arran centuries ago, over his father's protests. Oh, now there was a familiar feeling—the baffled anger and grief that the people he loved could not see things as clearly as he could see them.

"I've been Arran's friend a long time," he corrected her, watching with interest the hurt look in her eyes, the way she bent her head and curtained her reaction with jewels. "Not yours." He levelled the rod, felt a bit like Harry Potter at the pose and was about to say "how do I work this thing" when he felt the intention to act travel down his arm, down the bone and leap across the empty air like a spark. The cage shuddered once more and the carven leaves tinkled against their frame. That was all, he thought at first, until he'd stared long enough to see Sumala breathe. *My sister, and my rival. What the hell am I supposed to feel?*

"I want to hear from her why my father disowned me," Ben said, allowing the shadow personality who knew what was going on to speak. "I have the feeling... I remember. A little. That it was your fault."

He almost wished he could turn over the whole conversation to this side of himself he'd never known before and didn't trust. It would be easier than having to watch as Geoff rubbed his eyes, stretched. The man looked so stupid in his float vest and flying jacket. He looked like a cliché of an airman, except that in the films they had fewer stains, fewer rips in the leather sewn carefully back together by someone with a darning needle and lots of patience. Thinner, shabbier than what Hollywood would have provided.

Geoff opened his eyes, looked to be having some problems focussing, that screen-idol face of his full of the same struggle with ghostly dreams and memories Ben felt in himself. For a moment his eyes seemed yellow as those of the dragon that had attacked Ben, then he pinched them shut, rubbed his forehead and focussed, and they were blue. "*You?*"

"Who was it who told you to kill this man?" Oonagh asked while the two of them stared at each other and seemed equally lost for words.

Geoff looked away with a bitter smile, licked his lips. "I'm not required to give you that information. Glad to know I was told the truth about him being an agent in your pay, though."

Ben moved away, took a turn around the room, trailing his hand over the rough stone walls. It looked like a crypt, with its stubby pillars and the branching vaults above his head which held up the city. There were tapestries, but they were so thick with dust and faded with age he could barely see the ghost shapes of pale hunters on a pale background, riding down a pale stag.

Oh. Well, that explained things, just a little. Poor bastard. How long had Geoff been here anyway? How many lies had he been told already? Ben could, if he strained forgiveness to the limits, almost feel sorry for Geoff. He knew now, himself, what it was to feel completely at sea, lost for any firm ground to stand on, in doubt even of his own self.

"I'm not in anyone's pay," he said, aware this wasn't going to make things any easier for the man. "I'm some kind of reincarnation, if I understand it right, of someone who was an ally of hers in a previous life. In this life, I'd never heard of her or you until you tried to kill me."

Geoff frowned in confusion, then his face cleared. "How's the skipper?"

"Chris, you mean?" Not a subject Ben wanted to talk about, particularly not in front of an audience. "Fine. He's a pain in the neck, and I fully expect him to do something stupid and get in here somehow to rescue me."

"I wouldn't hold on to that thought too long."

Such a mix of feelings—it wasn't up to him to comfort the bastard. But it wasn't fair of Geoff to say such a thing. "He thought you were dead. They showed him a body, said it was you. He couldn't bring himself to examine it any closer. He only found out otherwise at the pool. And there...there we thought you were some kind of apparition. A ghost maybe, or else the Good People messing with his head for their own purposes. He's been planning to come ever since."

Geoff's lips whitened as he pressed them together. He looked away. Cleared his throat. "And you're not employed by the queen to do him harm?"

"That's what you were told?"

"Yes. I'm starting to think I've been led right down the garden path. It seemed to make sense at the time, because if you were innocently human, how could you be Sumala's brother?"

Ben turned to the woman in the cage. She was the most beautiful thing he had ever seen in his life. Part of him—the largest part—disapproved strongly of her costume. It was one thing for the Apsaras carved on temples to be filmily clad in gauzy skirts with their breasts, round as melons, revealed for all to see. Quite another for a real live person to wear such a getup. His mother would have been scandalised.

But presumably, in a different life, his other mother would have entirely approved, brushed the girl's long hair herself and tangled it with strings of gold. "You're really my sister? This is, well. Bizarre."

"It is just as strange for me," she said and reaching out, pulled at the cage door, making it rattle. There were tears in her eyes as she peered at him. "You are so human, it's horrible. How can you stand it?"

"I don't remember anything else."

"Still, it's cruel. I never thought our father was cruel, but then he did this to you, and he's left me here in this land of barbarians to be treated like a slave, and I'm beginning to think that he..."

"Why did he do it?" Ben asked, trying not to be overwhelmed by the jostle of someone else's concern in his head. So what if it was an older version of himself? He was using this body now, it could damn well remember it was a guest. But having said that, he was curious about this himself.

Sumala ducked her head until she was talking to her feet. "You don't remember?"

"I don't remember anything—I already said."

"It was because of Arran." Sumala was still mumbling, making Oonagh lean in to try to hear her, the queen's gaze fixed on her lips as though she could read the words from the shape.

"Because you two were…being perverted together…and you refused to give him up and get married as father commanded."

A flash of light burst inside Ben's head, expanding into a sphere of hot gold, and he remembered a courtyard full of glitter and sandalwood, domes so bright against the deep blue sky the dazzle should have blinded him.

"You owe me grandchildren. It is your duty."

"I owe you honesty."

"And obedience."

"Father, what is the reason why I cannot marry Arran? It would unite two kingdoms just as effectively, and now that we're working together to find new worlds…"

"You have no concept of dharma at all, do you, boy? Why will you have no pity for your own father? How can I pay my own debt to the gods—the debt I incur by my existence—if you will not put down this evil association and have children? Other worlds are nothing to me if you intend to damn your own father with your wickedness. Wretched child! I must punish you, if only to return you to your senses. Exile, I think. In the human world."

He remembered the absolute horror with disbelief. Remembered how the terror of such a fate had struck at his throat and his bowels, made him sick. How he had almost relented, almost given Arran up—almost given himself up and grovelled at the prospect. But both parts of him were proud that he had not, that in the end he had swallowed, straightened up and accepted it without flinching.

Then he had forgotten the whole thing, been left living a life meant as a punishment with no conception of what he had done to deserve it. And, frankly, it hadn't been that bad after all.

"My human father was a better man," Ben said, bitterly.

Oonagh curled herself into the throne on the dais. "I didn't know," she said, with a faint tone of apology. Like an underwater creature, her colour changed to match the stone. Her downcast eyes and drooping mouth might have been carved, a picture of regret. "You disappeared. We were told you had gone on retreat and did not wish to be found. All your subjects, I think, were told the same. Perhaps he hoped you would die soon, earn your place back and return before anyone would have cause to question."

"I loved Arran that much?" Ben felt slightly sick at the thought. He had enough romantic complications as it was. "It doesn't seem like me to be that serious over anyone."

Geoff gave him a glare. "Is that so?"

Oonagh smiled. "It is like you to refuse to give way under threat. I do not know what you felt for Arran, but your pride has never taken well to ultimatums." She raised her head and her moonstones gleamed like eyes. "I am thinking that it is clearly time for your father to consider his own spiritual well-being. He should retire to the forest to work out his debts to the gods. Kingship is full of toil and better suited to a younger man."

Bloody hell. This was too much to cope with. God knew what he'd expected, but being offered a past and a crown was not part of it, let alone the idea that he should snatch them both from the hands of his own father.

Staging a coup to take over a kingdom—that was so far from being his style he was inclined to laugh at the idea. But it was pretty obvious that if he played along with Oonagh's game while the first step was being prepared, he'd qualify as an honoured and trusted ally. He'd be given the same freedoms he'd enjoyed so far. With that freedom he could, perhaps, figure out what he wanted to do next and find a way to achieve it.

"This Chitrasen isn't the father I remember. Not the father to whom I owe reverence and thanks. So I'm not saying no to that idea. But I…I need time to think. Give me an hour or so alone? I'm not… This is a lot to take in."

"Of course." Oonagh unfolded herself and stood. He didn't think there was suspicion in her face, but it was difficult to be sure. "I'll have you escorted back to your rooms."

Ben took another look at the prisoners in the cage, his echo of a second soul furious and tender of Sumala's restraint, his own hating the sight of Geoff, hating himself because of it. "What about these two?"

"They can wake or sleep as you wish," said the queen. "But I will not have them released. Not yet. When you have remembered who you are and given me your word that you are my ally, as you once were, then we can discuss this decision."

"I'm supposed to be your champion." Geoff shook the bars again, filling the room with a sound like rain. "How can I do that from in here?"

Oonagh laughed. "In truth, this solution should have occurred to me earlier. If it is your destiny to be my champion, my champion you will be, even though locked in a box. Until such a time, you are a great deal less trouble in here. Shall we?"

She offered Ben her arm, led him away. He stopped at the door and looked back, found them watching him with the kind of wary, shell-shocked expression he imagined he wore himself. No need to fake the need to stop and think. He felt he would unravel like a weak seam if anyone spoke another word to him.

Returned to Arran's chambers, Ben walked a relentless circle around the walls. Arran was not there—a small mercy for which he was inclined to thank God. Sitting down was enough to throw open the lids on his mental confusion, letting everything stream out and swirl dizzyingly through his head. The doubt and disbelief were literally sickening. He could feel them in his stomach and at the back of his throat. The more he tried to pick them apart, make some sense of what he'd just learned, the more he felt he was going to throw up. He didn't want to see Arran again until he'd also had time to think through the *did we or didn't we* crawl in the flesh of that remembered something between them that might have been sex.

Shit, had Geoff been dealing with this kind of confusion for the last seventy-odd years? Unanchored, dislodged from anything he understood, estranged from anything he could rely on? If he had...

If he had, he would be the one person in this world who might give Ben a straight answer. Throwing on a cloak from the wardrobe, raising the hood over his face, Ben slipped back outside, retraced his steps. The wand still lay on the floor of the room where he had dropped it. Sumala sat cross-legged in meditation in the cage, and Geoff flinched, hiding something, trying to pretend he hadn't been attempting to pick the lock. His guilty look fell away when he saw Ben, to be replaced by something more complicated, but no less wary.

Feeling like a complete bastard, Ben pointed the wand at Sumala, switched her off. It felt like a sacrilege, and he was not surprised at the way Geoff backed away from him, his face hard. "I say! Was that really necessary?"

"I want to talk to you in private. It seemed the only way."

The cage was basic, large enough so that Geoff could pace from one side to the other, check the fit of the bronze bars into the stone of the floor. He sat down, leaning against them, stretching out long legs in scuffed soft flying boots. "I could murder a smoke."

"Sorry." Yielding to the change in the atmosphere, Ben grabbed the cushion off the throne, lowered himself to the ground too, leaning a shoulder on the bars. The buzzing tang—a kind of sugar-free mint taste—of the time field around Sumala filtered even into the half of the cage where Geoff sat, setting his teeth on edge. "I don't smoke. I can't offer you one."

What to say, now he had the chance? It seemed self-indulgent to talk about Chris, to stake claims neither of them had much chance of acting on.

It was Geoff who sighed, tipping back his head to rest on the bars. "So how long have you been in the Service?"

"Sorry?"

A quizzical look, the mouth tilted at one side. "At home, I mean. I'm assuming you've come over from India? Volunteered for the war effort. Lots of chaps from the Empire in the RAF, thank God."

For a moment, Ben was overcome with the urge to get up and wipe the dust from everything, take down that tapestry and beat it until the colours came through again, find a broom somewhere and spruce up the place until it shone. He recognised the urge as a way to stop thinking, to avoid emotion and decision. His mouth felt as gritty as though he had actually tried it when he said, "You still think it's the forties, don't you?"

Hard to tell in the dim underwater light of the place, but he thought Geoff's face paled before the man raised his jacket collar in both hands and tipped his face into it. "It isn't?"

"No. It is...was 2011 when I was brought here." There was an abyss of a thought. He had no more idea than Geoff did whether it was *still* 2011. It might already be a hundred years in the future and too late.

"And the war?"

"Long over. Oh, and we won."

"God." If Geoff had been standing, he would have staggered, lowered himself to his knees. It showed in the tremble of his hands as he bowed his head into them, gasped softly, as though he'd been hit in the stomach. "You're telling me the truth? So help me God, if you aren't..."

"I'm sorry."

"That's why he's older. The skipper, I mean. They didn't drain him of the time. I've just been in here for twenty years."

"Not twenty," Ben corrected, gently. It didn't seem a time for petty jealousy, when he was watching a man be destroyed in three easy blows. "Closer to seventy."

Geoff's hopeless look made him smile, one of those shamefaced smiles people give when they know it hurts and can't do a thing to change it. "It's complicated. He's displaced in time too, but he came back to earth fifteen years ago, and has been living in normal time ever since."

Ben took a breath, and he was surprised how much he hurt, surprised by his own thought that there wasn't much to go back to if he was going to be all self-sacrificial about this. But he still said it. "Fifteen years isn't much, after all. And you should have seen him when he found out you were alive—like every Christmas come at once."

Geoff's tragic look was startled into a smirk, but it faltered immediately and died. Putting his hand in one of the pockets of his overalls, he scooted closer and passed Ben a little pouch of leather that felt squishy in his hand. Geoff's touch was firm and businesslike, but that matinee-idol face wore a look of misery too profound for any hero. "Be that as it may. I have to trust someone, and if the skipper trusts you then that's as good as a pass in my book. I shouldn't have let myself get distracted because there's more at stake here than just us."

He rubbed a hand through stringy, unwashed hair and scowled. "Oonagh is raising an army," he said quietly. "I've been told it's an invasion army. I understand now why...my contact in the resistance...wanted you dead. You're obviously a key link in Oonagh's plans. Now that she has you, the time must be getting short. We have to tell Chris it'll be any day now. He should tell the authorities. You heard all that business about pollution?"

"I did. But Oonagh claims her plan is to leave this world altogether and look for a new one."

"And my informant tells me that her plan is to leave this world and take ours. You should see the army. I don't believe for a moment she'd muster a force like that and intend peace."

Ben remembered, suddenly, the wood in which he had crashed to land—the wood full of armour, the sense he'd had of being watched by hostile eyes, though he'd never caught a sight of them. And they were camped just outside the place where he'd come through to this world, waiting for the order. "Shit!"

Geoff's eyebrows went up and his mouth quirked. Ben remembered that he came from a more genteel time. But he only said, "Quite. Pester the queen for some cigarettes for me, would you?"

Ben laughed. He quite liked the guy, truth be told, and that made it all a hell of a lot worse. Still romance could take a backseat for the moment in favour of the question of how to get out of here alive. He worked the knot loose and opened the pouch he'd been given, frowning at the contents. "If I get the chance. So what's this?"

"Ah." Geoff reached through the bars to lay fingertips carefully on the small bag of dirt. "That's how you talk to the skipper. Throw a little pinch into still water. You've got to say a rhyme over it, ask for him. Then you'll be able to see him, in the reflection, like a magic mirror. You'll need something to write on—sound doesn't get through, unless you're both in the same world."

Ben squished the thing in his fingers. "What happens if you throw the whole lot in?"

"I don't know." Geoff was clutching at his hair again, bowed over grief as if it was a stomachache. "But there's a portal where a handful of this will break the barrier between worlds and you can walk across."

"And you haven't?"

The little unhappy grin again. "We were caught, just at the last moment. Hence the cage. I'd say talk to the skipper first. Plan it. If he's on the other side with a machine gun when the queen's forces roll up, you'll have a lot better chance of making it through."

All of a sudden Ben had a flash on the Great Escape, realised with a strange wringing twist of regret and guilt and nostalgia that Geoff had gone all escape committee on him, as though it was a foregone conclusion that only one of them was getting out alive. Geoff dropped his gaze, as if he saw it too and was embarrassed. "If you can bring me paper, I can draw you a map."

He was about the same age as Ben, but he had the weary, beaten eyes of a man three times as old.

"What about you? Sumala?"

"We'll manage. There's still a war on, after all. Or there will be soon. More important things to think about."

"Shit."

Geoff laughed again, covering his eyes with a hand. "My sentiments exactly." He waved the other hand in Sumala's direction. "Wake her up before you go, would you? She's the brains of the outfit, and her father may help if we can get to him."

"You think?" Ben had no time for parents who disowned their own children, doubly so when the child was himself.

"Worth a try, isn't it? We're not brimming over with options. Unless you happen to have a key to this cage in your coat and a spare army in your pocket?"

"I'm sorry," Ben said again, acknowledging the point, trying to get across his regret that things should be as they apparently were. I'm sorry was about the only thing that could cover it. "Well, good luck then."

Geoff gave a complex smile. "You too. And look after him for me."

Ben almost said something flippant, God forgive him, out of sheer habit. He caught himself in time with a shock and nodded instead, serious, focussed, tucking the pledge away like the sacred trust it was.

He'd been swamped in doubt, before, but a moment's conversation with a fellow human being and he knew exactly where he stood. Reincarnation be damned, he was Ben Chaudhry now, and that was the only thing that mattered.

It could have been reassuring, Chris thought, picking his way between the brambles that had overgrown his garden path, to discover that he had begun to feel confident and at home in this decade. He must have done, mustn't he, for the arrest and the time in a cell to feel so shattering. If he'd been uprooted and shoved straight back to the insecurity and unreality of his first weeks in the nineties, it must show that he'd begun to put down roots. They couldn't have been severed as they just had been, unless they'd been there in the first place.

It continued to rain, the drifting, light drizzle that floats beneath umbrellas, that clings and soaks into every surface. He thought for a moment that the path was flooded at the end, until his foot crunched on broken glass. Fragments of his sitting-room window now formed a wide puddle beneath it. The hole where it should have been looked dark, except for the shards, still hanging on by threads of putty. Inside, he could see that someone had smashed the TV and spray painted *Murderer* on the wall in dramatic red paint. He looked down, his head bowed by the weight of care. *God, this is too much. Who chose me to be the scapegoat of the universe? Isn't it enough to ruin my life once? It has to be done on a regular basis every ten years?*

The shards of window overlapped each other in the grass, slicked with the continuing downpour. He looked at them numbly, just as something stirred behind them. Somewhere between the water and the glass, between the glass and the grass beneath it, Ben looked out from another world.

"Shit!" The relief was so intense it made his skin feel as if it had been rubbed all over with chilli—a kind of hot/cold tingle so intense as to be almost painful. "Shit. Ben, oh thank God."

Ben looked all the more like the prince of his dreams, clad in peacock silk with emeralds around his neck and wrists, and a pearl-inlaid sword belt buckled around his waist, but there was something shattered and fragile about his expression that matched the broken glass.

Heedless of the damp, Chris splashed to his knees in the mud of his garden, hunting through his pockets. Pen, yes. Paper? He found a bus ticket, wrote in large letters *R U OK?* and held it up.

Ben had come prepared. He grinned, looked away, and scratched a reply on the top of a long sheet of parchment. *Yes. Invasion imminent. You must tell someone.*

Already done took the back of the ticket, but further searching of the bins outside the front door—tricky when he didn't wish to take his eyes off Ben in case the connection was lost—netted him a pizza box, that folded inside out and gave him ample space. *I will come for you. Think I can reopen the place where you were taken. Can you go back to transfer point on your side?*

Ben ran the emerald necklace through his fingers as if it were worry beads. *I think so. They trust me—long story.* He still wasn't looking in Chris's face. He dipped his quill, fiddled with the feather. *Geoff is here.*

A stab of something unrecognisable and that feeling of too much sensitivity grew until he felt flayed, every drop of water against his face a torment of hope and despair. *You've seen him?*

Spoke to him yesterday. He's fine. Ben finally looked up, smiled, all challenge and bullshit like his old self. *I hate him.*

Chris laughed, the first time in a week, and something wild and giddy started up in his stomach, blue-white and tasting of oxygen neat out of the bottle. *Can you bring him?*

I'll try.

Good lad. Time, how did you synchronise time between the two universes? Ah... *Just get there, OK? I'll get the passage open. It'll be early tomorrow if I'm lucky, but check back, yes? Check in tomorrow and we'll take it from there.*

Shadows under Ben's eyes, and the rain slid across his smile like tears. *Will do.* He put the paper down, worried the necklace a little more, bright green flashes like sun through leaves between his fingers. Then he looked up, like a man determined to do a frightening task despite the cost, just as long as he could get it over with, and he said something. Chris watched his mouth move. It could have been "I love you," but he couldn't be sure. The pen creaked in his fingers and cracks ran up the plastic casing. He didn't know what to say. He'd have said it back, like a shot, if it wasn't for Geoff. But if Geoff was alive, if he really was alive and fine, didn't that change everything?

Ben's smile faltered. Chris reached down for the image of him—he looked so close there, as if he were standing in a grave beneath Chris's garden, and Chris could reach in and pull him out. But when his fingers touched the glass, there was only water. "I love you too," he said, but there was only water and grass to hear it. Damn it. Another perfect opportunity missed. What the hell was the matter with him?

The war had trained him well in pushing down his emotions and getting on with the necessary actions despite them. He got up, vainly tried to brush the knees of his trousers dry and went inside to where his living room was already smelling of damp and cats. There would be time to figure out what to do with two true loves when they were both safe.

He took the phone from its socket in the hall and went upstairs to change into dry, dark clothing. Phyllis answered after two rings.

"How d'you feel about being an accomplice to robbery?" he asked, and she laughed. He could hear her drawing her chair up to her telephone table, pulling out notebook and pen.

"Fire away. Oh, and by the way, Stan came to me yesterday with a new device he'd rigged up on your say-so. I took him back up to the Nine Ladies last night to test it out, and we may have something for you. I'll bring it with me to show you. I'm guessing you don't want me to rope him in for this?"

"You're quite right. I'm not having Stan involved in anything illegal. If he's really found something to help, that's more than enough. You can call Grace, though, if you like. Here's the plan..."

Ben mopped the pool of water from the room's black, reflective floor with his brief moment of certainty dissolved into a swirl of dismay. He moved into the large central chamber of Arran's rooms and pulled his finery over his head. The suit, in which he had been pulled through the earth into Faerie, had been laundered and repaired, not a trace of dirt on it and all the rents and tatters sewn up so finely they looked like they'd almost grown back together. He had found it when he returned, folded neatly on one of the firm cushions used for reclining by the fire pit on winter nights. Now he put it back on with a feeling of revulsion that he wasn't sure was his own. Such drab garments! Was he really giving up on the idea of a kingdom of his own in order to run back to a world where he had never fitted? What made that place so attractive now, other than habit and sentiment?

He tried not to allow the question to come into focus in his mind. Better not to think about that. Better not to be pushed around by creatures he didn't trust and understood only far enough to know their actions were motivated by their own agenda, not his. At least on earth he knew what other humans thought.

Or did he? How often had he felt the eternal outsider? All his life. And now he knew why. Because he had been living in an alien world, in exile. Had his differences, his heritage, always shown through? Would he always be as homeless there as he was here? Here at least he could storm his country and force them to recognise him. Back on earth...

He tied his tie carefully and smoothed it down. There was still no sign of Arran, so he could put the all-concealing cloak over everything and slip out into the nobles' quarter unobserved. His heritage didn't want him, after all, and he'd found a ragtag bunch of eccentrics at home who did. That was something to hold on to. Just because Chris couldn't bring himself to say the words—because he would be taking up with his old mate as if nothing had happened—did not mean there wasn't someone out there for Ben. This crumpling, tight feeling in his chest would wear off in time, he was sure.

He walked boldly through the evening crowd and down into the queen's undercity. Sumala and Geoff looked up at him with more desperate eyes this time, sharper faces, and he wondered if anyone had remembered to feed them, since no one but the queen knew they were here.

"We have to get you out. Does either of you know how to work this?" He brought the ivory wand out of his pocket and showed it to them.

"I do." Sumala extended her hand through the wire, and he dropped the thing into it just as footsteps sounded on the stairs outside, the heavy slither of something dragging down each riser.

"Shit," said Ben. "Chris thinks he can open the gate. Quick! Get out, you've got to come with me."

The light of torches had begun to spill around the corner, and the soft footfalls grew closer. Sumala looked at the door, bit her lip and then shook her head, passing the wand to Geoff. "Hide it. Not now."

"We must! There's three of us, we can knock them down and run."

Geoff thrust the wand into one of his many pockets. The door creaked farther open. Oonagh stood in the doorway, wearing body armour and a long split skirt of leather. She had a trident in one hand and in the other a crown. She looked at them all through eyes that were currently as purple as violets and tilted her head a little to the side. Even to himself, Ben's companions looked suspicious, like conspirators caught plotting.

Oonagh could hardly have missed Geoff wiping the sweat from his hands on his trousers or the fountainlike tinkle of Sumala's bells that betrayed her trembling. But she only said, "Ah, Karshni, well met. When I did not find you at your lodgings, I thought you must be here. It was your custom, when you visited us before, to go riding before sleep. I have sent Arran away for the moment because I desired to know you better myself, and I thought perhaps you would consent to accompany me instead?"

She watched his gaze be snagged by the crown and held it out with a little flourish as if offering cake to a child. It was indeed a beautiful thing, the silver circlet was narrow as a fingertip and carved all down its length with a design of two horses facing one another, their front legs interlaced. A single white gem in the centre shone of its own light like a star, and light floated between her fingers as she offered it to him, like tendrils of blood in water.

"It is fitting that a prince should wear a crown. I will not have anyone say of me that I do not know how to rightly honour my guests. Take it, and wear it so that my own people will know to do you reverence."

Ben looked from the jewel, not liking the sheen of it, up into her face. Who could tell what was going on behind those changeable eyes? He thought about how much he'd assumed, taken for granted. What was she really? She put on shapes and took them off as another person might change clothes. He'd been assuming he understood her, but why had he ever thought that?

She watched him hesitate, and those Disney heroine eyes narrowed in an expression no cartoon character could ever replicate. He had a strange flash of Arran, and that moment in the man's chambers where he had felt his flesh shift like water under his fingers. He shivered. No, he understood nothing. So this was the point to lash out? To fight? He could try to get the jump on her before she could use the trident that gleamed with sharpness in her right hand. Knock her out, take the others and run.

And have all of Faerieland on his tail? No, better play for time, play along and retain the freedom he'd been given thus far. "Thank you," he said, and took the thing.

It even felt shiny in his fingers. Light welled up and overspilled his hands. He raised the circlet and set it on his head, and the last thing he saw was Oonagh smiling, Sumala rattling the bars and yelling "No!" before a blinding flash of revelation struck him and all his problems and doubts fell away. It was the best thing that had ever happened to him, and he wished it had happened a thousand years before.

"There's a rescue plan," he said, laughing internally at the unfinished, raw-edged shape of it. How could anyone expect such a thing to work? He ignored the furious silence from the cage, Geoff's poisonous glare and thinned lips. "There's a man coming to rescue me. He'll open the portal in a matter of hours."

Oonagh tilted her head and looked at him, curious, wary. "That's not possible. Only a queen of Faerie can open the way between worlds, and that way has been shut for years. You and this one here are the only travellers who have been through since my foremothers' days."

"Maybe he's found a way you don't know about," Geoff put in, as if driven beyond caution by the need to defend his friend. "He's the other one in your prophecy, after all. The pilot. You know about as much about what he's capable of as you do about me."

It was bombast, pure and simple, Ben thought, not worthy of a response. But Oonagh took off the long string of diamonds that dangled from her throat and knotted it into a ball that flickered with pale colours between her fingers. She unknotted it again, and he understood that she had unknotted her thoughts, made a decision. "We will go and see him then, this pilot. At last, all the strands are coming together. The river speeds towards the waterfall, and what will be left of us, after the drop?"

"I can't believe I'm doing this," Grace whispered as she rounded the strut of the wheel, flicking the asperge to make a spray of holy water spatter the undercarriage of the plane.

"Shh!" Phyllis whispered back from where she had pulled away the chocks. In the dim red light of their infrared lantern, she looked up at Chris in the cockpit and gave a thumbs-up. The three of them were all but invisible in black coats and dark trousers, though the implement in Grace's hand glittered and the spray of holy water twinkled even in the midnight gloom.

"We're going to be put away for years." Finishing her blessing, Grace capped the flask in which she'd brought the water, tucked it away and grabbed one of the carbon-fibre ropes they had clipped to the plane. Chris jumped down from the wing and joined them at the ropes. With all three of them pulling, the replica de Havilland Mosquito began to roll silently forwards towards the doors. They passed the crowbar Grace had left lying in the centre of the path, the plane following, silently, rolling forward like a great ghostly moth.

Grace nudged Chris's elbow and said, again, "Are you sure about this?"

"If I can't do it in this, I can't do it at all." He looked at the girls and wondered why they seemed so grim. This part was the fun part, and he felt reckless and gleeful as he hadn't felt for years. Just like that time he'd tried to roll the Lanc to touch the steeple of Ely cathedral with the tip of one wing. High stakes just made it better.

"I hate to mention it, but it's not a Lancaster." Phil dropped out for a moment's rest as they passed the drowsing trainers and began to circle to bring the plane beneath the airfield's fuel bowser.

Chris looked up at the sleek and beautiful shape behind him, twin propellers at head height, the pilot's nacelle set between them, so the lucky man got to sit between two buzz-saw-like blades and hope like hell that nothing went wrong. "I know. There's no way we could have got the Battle of Britain Lanc, and I couldn't have flown it on my own if we had. I'd need my crew."

A clear, cold night, and the smell of dope and aviation fuel brought it all back, tightened it around his throat like a noose. On a night like this, it was as though he could step from one time to another. They were so close he could almost hear their

113

voices. "I wish...I wish the boys were here. I'd feel a hell of a lot more confident with them at my back."

The skin along his spine prickled with chill and yearning and eeriness, and he shrugged it off with some impatience. "But I'm sure they're looking down on me now and wishing me well. Without them, this is my better option. Love the Lanc like a brother, but this? Nothing like it in the world, at the time. Still isn't, for me."

Getting the fuel in the plane called for a great deal more climbing than he'd done in years, and the girls stood around at the bottom of the tower, stealing glances towards the security guard's office. He was fast asleep thanks to one of Phil's tranquillisers slipped into his tea, but none of them knew who might be coming to check on him or when his shift changed.

"Go," Chris said, clambering down to ground level once more. "Go now and get long gone before I start this thing up. There'll be an almighty racket, and you don't want to be seen leaving the premises at that point."

"Hold your horses." Phil fumbled in her haversack and brought out a sandwich bag full of dirt. She tipped it out onto her palm and let the wind sieve the dry earth away. What emerged, slowly, was a blink of gold and then a glitter. A curved side embellished with tiny dots. When she shook the last of the dirt off, the thing made a low, dim tinkle, and he saw it was a tiny bell, scrunched up to close its singing mouth.

Phil handed it to him as though it was as delicate as a snowflake. "This is what Stan and I found. It was buried deep down in a rabbit's burrow, but you should have seen how it lit up the detector. Like a...like a fusion reactor of magic, or so Stan said. There's a coarse dust inside it. One or two flecks escaped and even they were like little galaxies. We don't know what it does, but we're sure it does something that takes a lot of magic to do."

Chris looked down on it—a fragile and beautiful thing. A thing of power. Tipping the dust into his palm, he rubbed it along the nose, propellers and wings of his plane. He had no idea what he was playing with, but it could hardly hurt his chances.

Let's face it, the whole venture was a bloody stupid idea, and in all likelihood tonight would be the last night of his life. A couple of hours flying before he was nose-diving into a field, and he'd know then, one way or another, whether any of this worked. That...didn't feel at all bad, now he came down to it. It felt blue-white like a master searchlight when the blaze seemed to consume you and strip your flesh from your bones, leaving you naked.

He rubbed the back of his neck where the wool of his old jacket was proving that it had hardened and gone brittle sharp over the last fifteen years. What did you say? It was easy on ops because you were taking the chaps with you, because routine dulled the edge of it and everyone knew what the words were that had been left unspoken. He wasn't sure the silent intercom was working for these two. "Well, wish me luck."

"You don't even know what you're doing." That was Grace, looking ferocious in her balaclava, but with terrified eyes. "What if it doesn't work?"

"Then it'll be your job to stop them, I'm afraid. So buck up and get moving."

They both looked at their feet. He hoped they weren't going to say something sentimental. But the seconds ticked in silence and eventually Phil offered him her hand and a wrought-iron smile. "See you on the other side."

"Good luck, Chris."

"Thank you. Okay then, I'll give you ten minutes to get away. Starting now."

He watched them go with a kind of shameful relief. Good. All that awkwardness set his teeth on edge. There was time to smoke a single cigarette and look up at the stars. Propping himself against the wing, he smoked quietly, watched the curlicues of vapour wind up into the high, light cloud, and thought about the boys gone before him into the dark. Perhaps some of their ghosts would be riding with him tonight. The thought gave him an ache of nostalgia and some comfort.

Yielding to the whimsy of the moment, he ducked his head and whispered, soft as the exhale of blue smoke into his palm. "If you're there, chaps, if you're listening, I could do with some help. Hop aboard, and I'll give you the ride of your deaths."

He ground out the cigarette on its case and tucked the butt into his pocket for fear of leaving DNA evidence. With a final sigh, he swung up through the entry dock and thence into the cockpit. It smelled perfect, and all the dials were as he remembered, painted in phosphorescent paint. Just as well, as the street lighting seemed to have gone out. The lights of every house around the aerodrome had switched off as though all their occupants had decided to flee the witching hour together. Beneath the wheels of the plane, a soup of darkness moved, eddying and billowing to its own breeze.

Chris's skin prickled again—the thought of ghosts no longer quite so amusing. Swallowing down fear like an ice cube, he went through his preflight checks methodically. The engines coughed and spluttered, jets of fire licking from the exhausts. Then they caught and burst into a solid euphonious roar. He applied full brake and throttled the engines up to max. A jolt went through the airframe just as if, once again, someone had pulled away the chocks, and when he looked down he saw a blue uniformed figure with only half a face. With a salute, the ghostly erk melted back into the dissipating burst of start-up smoke.

Chris wondered for a moment if it was raining, if water was fogging the Perspex, but no, it was tears, tears he was scarcely aware of shedding as he let go the breaks and the little plane hurtled into the sky, its fuselage humming like a pipe organ. The bone-shaking rattle and roar down the runway and then she kissed off the ground and was climbing, undercarriage folding away, and it was sweet and weightless and exultant, and he had to press his eyes into the inside of his elbow to wipe the tears away long enough to see.

God, they'd heard him! All this time—after all this time—and they'd come because he needed them.

"Who's with me, then?"

"All of us, Skipper." He'd brought his helmet too, plugged it into the intercom during preflight checks out of habit. He choked now on his own sob as the whisper sounded in his ear. The faint dry tang of the Yank's voice.

"Did you piss on the wheels for luck?" That sounded like Red in the rear gun turret. God, he'd forgotten how much he missed that little, ambiguous hint of mockery in the smooth tones, as though Red had cocked the inevitable snook at death and was very pleased with himself as a result.

"Couldn't in front of the ladies," he whispered back, and the phantom voice chuckled.

"We're doomed… Oh, wait. Old news, right?"

In the absence of a navigator, Chris picked up the line of a motorway on the ground below, silver as a stream in the light of a bomber's moon. There was an Arctic chill running down his back and his mouth tasted of tin, but it was better to have these things out, straightaway. "Have you come to collect me?"

"You're not allowed to ask things like that," said Tolly's adenoidal voice, sounding desperately young.

"He's allowed to ask, we're not allowed to answer," Red corrected.

"Are you really there, or am I imagining this?"

"That one too."

"Unhelpful as you ever were, I see." Chris flew through cloud, and in the sudden pitch dark, he thought he saw them for a moment, glimmers like lines of phosphorescence in the air. But then the Mosquito climbed above the vapour and the moon shone bright into an empty cabin. Though his heart felt light as froth, he still shivered. "Less chitchat, then. Let's do this."

Chris flew low, hugging the ground. It was highly unlikely that any of the local air-traffic radar stations would pick him up—the Mosquito's wooden construction made it less likely to detect. But low flying minimised that risk even further, as well as reducing the chance of collision with something shuttling along the unknown network of commercial flights stacked up through the stratosphere above him. It also allowed him to see where he was going—to navigate by landmarks as he'd done in the old days. And just as importantly, it was more fun this way. If this was his last flight, it might as well be a good one. If it wasn't—if by some strange miracle he survived—then the repercussions from a joyride in a stolen plane were likely to be the least of his problems.

So he gave the memory of those Spitfire boys with their arrogance a thorough thrashing, turning side on to scrape through below Cottingly aqueduct and giving the poachers in the fields the fright of their lives.

Perhaps it was one of them who phoned up to report him or perhaps he had simply crossed into the range of Manchester Airport's more powerful radar, but he had just begun to recognise the shapes of the Peaks below when the radio burst into life, cutting through the band-saw throb of the engines.

"Unidentified aircraft, you have no clearance to be in this airspace. Identify yourself."

Chris opened his mouth and shut it again, knowing that there was nothing he could say. The line of the Bakewell road peeled off from the motorway below him, and he altered course to follow it.

"Unidentified aircraft, respond." Even through the sound of his own engines, he could hear the higher, more machinelike drone of something on his tail. In seconds they had idled up on either side of him, two Eurofighter Typhoons, having some trouble in going as slowly as he.

"Let me shoot them down." That was Occe, who hadn't seemed to have registered that he was flying in a famously unarmed bomber.

"What with?" he asked, just as Tolly—wireless operator—spoke directly to the pursuing pilots, giving the call sign for good old V for Victor.

"Boys, we're not..." Ah! And now he could see the field in the distance, the standing stones looking almost yellow in the light of the big bone moon.

The pilot in the lead Typhoon had swung his plane close enough so he could have stepped from his wing onto Chris's. His face was clear as day, shadowed eyes grim beneath his helmet shield. "You'll accompany us back to base and surrender your vehicle. If you fail to comply, we are authorised to shoot you down."

"I can get him from here." Red joined the call to be allowed to use his beloved guns. Chris wriggled in his seat, looked over his shoulder, and just for moment in the dark thought that he saw the main spar of a Lanc behind him and the body behind it receding into the distance like a corridor. Swallowing, he looked out of the cockpit and saw wider wings, four engines outlined in cobweb light. For that same moment, the weight on the stick was punishing, the feeling of the plane beneath him magnificent, the heavy, brutal, beautiful beast he had flown in his youth.

He got a fix on the stone beneath which he had found Ben's phone. The scored ground under it was invisible in the night, but he remembered—a little hole about the size of a badger's set, ringed with grass and filled with crumbling soil and worms.

Turning to put it dead ahead of him, he saw moonlight on *Victor*'s four engines, and beneath his feet, the back of Archie's head where he sat in a bomb nacelle that hadn't existed for seventy years.

Chris would have thought it was just that he was going mad, if both Typhoon pilots had not reared back in their cockpits and peeled off to twice the distance, making room in the sky for a far bigger plane. A crackle of shocked expletives burst from his earpiece and then even the background noise of radio contact cut off for a moment.

He felt sorry for them, truly. The pair of them were looking at each other. He could imagine them confirming that the other guy really was seeing what he was seeing. Even now they would be working their way past the sinking realisation that there was a form to fill in back at base that had no space on it for ghostly kites from the war, still thundering across the countryside to rain their nightly terror on Germany.

"Unidentified aircraft, you will accompany us to base or we will shoot you down. Acknowledge."

Chris shut off the radio, cut off their voices and as easily dismissed them from his mind. "Good work, chaps," he told his crew. "And thank you. I don't know if you still obey my orders, being dead, but time to bail out. I'll see you on the other side."

"Always were a joker, Skip." The voice made him jump. Right beside him, elbow to elbow. Hank's voice, with a little crackle to it as if recorded on vinyl that had not been handled gently over the years. "This is our fight too, remember? We've had to wait a very long time to get our own back against these bastards. We're not scrubbing out now."

"Brace yourselves, then."

He moved the throttle forwards, the touch of cold, clammy fingers over his own, lending their strength. Putting the plane into a long, shallow dive, he aimed the nose at the base of the hill, where the tiny scrape in the soil was a closed door into another world. Speed picked up, the dial of the altimeter spinning down to zero. The two grey fighters, unprepared for the move, zipped past, then turned in tight curves, vapour streaming from their wingtips as they doubled back. There'd be more swearing going on in those cockpits, Chris thought with a flash of manic laughter as the blur of the earth rushed at him. The undercarriage touched one of the standing stones and yellow sparks flew as he was thrown against his straps, but he lifted her off and rammed her into the ground. *Open wide, I'm coming through.*

Everything blurred, black and grey. There was an immense rushing noise. He thought he heard the crash, aluminium buckling under impact, the tinny shriek of fuselage being torn apart, the trickle of fuel and then the *whoomph* as it caught the sparks and exploded. He closed his eyes, just for a second, and there was—God, there *was* burning, eviscerating light behind them, making his eyelids shine crimson.

But his breath went on, ragged and fast over a thundering heartbeat. He snapped his eyes open, pulled back on the stick just in time to bring the nose up. The tail dragged a thin furrow in water edged with reeds, and by the time he'd levelled off it was over a riverbank, bordered in grass as green as in a child's painting and backed by a forest of elm and elder under strong, bluish sunlight. Against all probability he had made it through. He had arrived.

Chapter Six

Chris circled above the grassy field, looking frantically for the way back. Was there a slightly more steel tint to the water just beside that thin wooden causeway where it was ringed in bullrushes? Perhaps. And there were bullrushes decorating the damp wings, splattered like insects across the Perspex of the cockpit. "You still with me, lads?"

"Still here, Skipper." Their voices sounded fainter. There was an echo to them, as though they came distantly down a long corridor where a stormy wind blew.

"But where are our rescuees?" Chris lined up for a landing, lost speed, came down, floating, floating and then the ah, the breathless turbulent bone-shaking rush of the wheels kissing ground: potholes and rabbit holes, mole hills and stones, and the edge of the forest rushing up towards him like a green and grey wall. The flaps caught, the brakes caught, he swung the nose of the plane around to position for an immediate takeoff, and then taxied slowly to a halt. He'd caught something moving out of the corner of his eye. In the forest, wasn't it?

Unbuckling his straps, he shifted round in the seat to look behind him. There the trees grew so thick he saw no undergrowth at all. Two paces in and the bright day had been so thoroughly snuffed he saw only floating stars where a stray beam had found a tiny crack in the leaf cover. Floating stars and other, darker things, moving. The skin along his spine itched as a ruff he didn't have tried to stand on end.

There were eyes in there. The bluish gleams were not leaf-dappled light at all, but a phosphorescence at the back of night hunter's eyes. There was a pulling in and shifting, as if the trees had turned into liquid, hit the ground and splashed back up as something else. Light began to penetrate as the tree cover thinned, and with every second he could see the process more clearly—falling branches becoming figures in armour, shield and sword in hand. He had flown not onto a deserted plain but right into the middle of a waiting army.

He pressed contact for the engines again, throttled them up, was beginning to ease away when a small boat rounded the corner of the river ahead of him, brushing past purple and yellow irises, scattering the waterfowl from beneath its curved prow. Despite the cockroach-like crawling of the woods behind him, there was a moment of triumph, of relief as sharp as a stab wound. He turned off the engines and scrambled out.

Bright as a ruby in crimson silk, crowned with a silver circlet, Ben guided the boat to the shore, leapt out, his movements sure and flowing. Chris stopped, hunkered down on the wing of the plane, arrested by the expression on the young man's face, the way he moved—the certainty, poetry and arrogance of it.

He tried to cough out the dread that had settled like cold water in his lungs and shouted, "Ben! Quick! Get in!"

But it was like that moment in nightmares—he knew what was coming, and that made it more horrifying rather than less. Ben strolled over to the plane, put a hand on the wing next to Chris's foot and looked him in the face, and Chris felt he was looking at a man he'd never met before. "Ben?"

"You wondered what I was. Didn't you? The others never quite let go their feeling that I might not be trustworthy. That I might not be fully human."

"But you *are*!" Chris leaned down, took hold of Ben's arm and tugged. It certainly felt as human as ever, but for the slippery sleeve, dotted with seed pearls and silver. "At any rate, come on. This is not a good time for discussion."

Ben's brow creased. The too-wide, too-certain eyes clouded over. He looked away from Chris to what seethed behind the plane. Following his gaze, Chris saw that the first armoured phalanxes of an army were spilling out of the trees onto the riverbank. They were drawing up in ranks, all clad in green and grey, their banners rolled around their spear shafts and tied tight.

It was a very different look Ben gave him next—clever, doubtful, wary—a very Ben kind of look. It made Chris lean down, take a hold of Ben's filigreed platinum belt and try to lift him bodily into the plane. "They're with you?" Ben asked.

"Not me. I thought they were with you. You've landed on your feet here, I see." Ben hung from his aching hands. The muscles in his back stretched and burned and would not answer his demand to contract, to pull the dangling man bodily off the floor. "Come on, damn it! Give me some help here."

A moment's more uncertainty. Ben's face creased as though he was in pain. He reached up his other hand, but it had scarcely brushed Chris's sleeve before he dropped it again, the tiny muscles around his eyes changed, second by second, as though he fought a war in there. "I...don't..."

The sound of the afternoon shifted as a great sibilant *sssh* Chris had taken for the brush of the wind over the treetops detached itself from the background noise, grew heavier, louder, more regular. At the same time, there came a noise like cymbals and a distant, bell-like voice over the wind. Ben's face transfigured with joy. It all but glowed as he reached up a second time and began to bend back Chris's fingers, prizing them away from his arm.

Looking for the source of the voice, for the thing that had made Ben's face shine, Chris saw it, coming in from the east. He'd never hoped to see one, never believed in them, but what went through him on seeing the spread, black, batlike wings, the long, lean body, trailing away in loops of tail, and the crocodile-like head, teeth aglitter, was instant recognition, fear and awe, and not a little glee. *Bloody hell, now I've seen everything!*

"I don't belong in your world, human. I belong here." Ben's fist struck Chris in the jaw, taking him by surprise, jamming his teeth into his tongue, filling his head with grey sparkles and his mouth with the taste of blood.

"Oh no you don't, you little...!" Both Chris's hands were occupied. He tried again to lift Ben off the ground. If he smacked Ben's head into the underside of the wing he might be able to stun him for long enough to get him aboard. But with Ben struggling, he managed only to haul him up a couple of feet and jam his shoulder at an awkward angle between two of the propeller blades.

"I am a prince of the Gandharva people. Unhand me or you will know my wrath!"

"It's a fucking rescue, you arse. Now get in the plane." But he knew by then that persuasion wouldn't do it. The Ben Chaudhry he knew—change of convictions or not—could never have uttered such a line with a straight face. Possession? Or was this some kind of clone? An evil twin?

Ben was twisting in his grip. Chris's shoulders were about to separate themselves from his body, he could feel the muscles pulling, ripping. That hissing grind grew louder with every panting breath. A moment's glimpse behind him showed a great white shape bulking out of the forest like the grinding of a glacier. Ice shone on its scales. The iron-fanged muzzle gaped as high as a house. It had made its way through the ranks of the army, was dragging itself into a catlike crouch. The membranes of its wings, blue-white as skimmed milk, stretched taut as it unfolded its wings.

On its back sat a woman in a robe of chain mail, so fine and flexible it might have been linen. The mask of her helmet gleamed like bright gold, her living eyes looking out eerily from the smooth metal. A chill went down Chris's back as she raised her spear and pointed at him.

His voice failed him. He had to whisper. "Ben. This is going straight to hell. If you're coming with me, do it now. Please."

The white dragon beat its wings once, testing them out. The blast of wind almost knocked Chris off his perch. He had to let go of Ben's arm to scrabble for purchase on the engine mounting, and as he did so, Ben drew a small, sharp knife from the top of his boot and stabbed it through the centre of Chris's other hand.

"Aaah!" he yelled, letting go involuntarily, the recoil throwing him back against the cockpit, hand cradled against his chest. "Ah. Ah. Oh fuck." It hurt. It hurt so much he could barely force his watering eyes to stay open, but he managed it, fumbling with edge of the entry dock behind him, getting it unlatched and open. It was enough to see Ben land lightly on both feet, run fast along the edge of the riverbank, his arms held out.

Above them, the black dragon folded its wings and plummeted like a stooping hawk. Its claws came down. It picked Ben up with careful delicacy, turned and began to beat back the way it came. Chris breathed through his clenched teeth, wiped his palm over his face to shake off tears and sweat, took one look at the way the white dragon was now clawing at the ground, beating steadily—for all the world like a fighter getting its engines to full power before releasing the breaks—and vaulted back into his seat.

Blood continued to pour from his hand, trickling between his fingers. He started up the engines, revved hard. The Mosquito began to trundle gently forwards. "Shit! Shit!" and he could have hated it for its elderly, arthritic slowness, but he didn't have the time, just poured all the power he could on, struggled to hold her steady and straight until he could feel the lift under the wings. The wheels bumped off the ground, and again, and then they were away in a shallow upward scrape, into an alien sky, and he had no idea which way to go, or where in the whole of this world he might be able to find Ben again, or Geoff.

He clipped the stiff leather of his oxygen mask to the side of his helmet, his good hand shaking, and the other still bleeding steadily, showing no sign of slowing or clotting. Clenched around the stick, it pulsed with a brilliant lemon-yellow pain. Once he had the oxygen flowing and could replace it with his other hand, it subsided to a dull, deep throb. The air mix helped him to get his breathing back under control, slow it from the rasping, back-of-the-throat pant, and it was a good thing it did, as he'd barely stopped hyperventilating before all the air in the cockpit seemed to disappear. The engines gave a shrill whine as the plane juddered, pulled backwards into a sudden vacuum.

The white dragon was in the air, the upstroke of its takeoff sucking the sky right out from beneath Chris's wings. The downstroke sent him bucking away on a whirlwind of turbulence, fighting the column with arms and legs, while the airframe of the plane shrieked in protest and the engines coughed and smoked. The rudder bar grew sticky beneath his feet as a wave of hot air pulsed through the plane from the tail. When he looked up, he could see green-gold fire lick along the Perspex, smoulder on the wooden blades of the propellers. He really didn't want to imagine what it was doing to the dope-painted dry wooden airframe of the plane.

Okay, scrub this as a rescue mission. It couldn't have gone any worse. All he could do now was get out of here, get some better intel and come back when there wasn't an entire army waiting for him. With a flash of panic, he saw the white dragon's pillar-like teeth at the window just in time. Sideslipping the gnash of its jaw, he banked around, scarcely more than head height. A burst of speed, a burst of height, and he dived straight for the smooth, mirrorlike water of the mere that was the portal on this side of the worlds. He felt it close over him; grey, black, and that moment that was like drowning and then he was out, climbing impossibly out of the side of the hill.

Elation hit him, just briefly—the joy of still being alive, of having escaped. He clenched his flying jacket tight, the leather softening beneath the still bleeding wound.

It was twilight, the silver-blue stillness of a world under a strong full moon, and he thought the tricky light was deceiving him for a moment, that the stir in the scrubby grass below was his own imagination. Then the snout of the dragon broke through, scattering earth. The long white wormlike body squirmed out onto a hillside near Bakewell, as early-morning lorries trundled with their lights on through the sleeping streets. The first rank of the army came after as he watched, as though a warriors' cemetery was emptying itself, mound by mound, disgorging shapes in silver armour, with helms and swords unsheathed in silver hands.

Chris rolled to a halt on the road. Sawing through his sleeve at the elbow with his pocketknife, he made a makeshift bandage while he watched them pour through the breach between worlds. *Jesus Christ Almighty! What to do?*

The woman on the dragon put up her helmet mask and looked at him. Nothing as sharply beautiful as that face should exist in this world. He heard her voice in his head like glass chimes even as she smiled her closed-lipped smile. *We have been waiting at the portal for some days now, but howsoever hard our greatest mages tried, we could not get through. Now you, by your own actions, have opened your world to us. Ironic eh?*

It was not perhaps the word he would have chosen himself.

Chapter Seven

"We've got to find the skipper before she does." Geoff scarcely waited until the queen's long skirt had swished round the archway of the door. Certainly her footsteps had not faded before he was pulling again at the interlacing metalwork of the cage, trying to untangle the individual strands of thin copper. It bent under his onslaught but would not part enough for him to slip a shoulder through.

"Stop that and give me the wand." Sumala touched his shoulder and it was as though he'd shocked himself on an electric light—a moment where he couldn't move even to breathe, and another, following, of racing heart, cold sweat and coughing.

He dug the thing out of his pocket as hurriedly as he could with benumbed and tingling hands and scowled. "Just asking politely would have done."

"I'm tired and hungry and I miss my home. I miss my country where I am a princess and free to do as I like, and never treated like this or spoken back to by rude commoners. And you are so stupid sometimes that I could cry..." Her voice trembled as she turned the wand over in her hands, pressed it to her forehead as if trying to see within it with her inner eye.

There was indeed a glitter of tears caught in her lashes, and her face had taken on a gaunt look, a thinness that added waiflike poignancy to her beauty, but that he should have realised was a sign of famine.

All at once he felt like a cad. "I'm sorry." She was, after all, a princess, and she'd been a complete brick over all of this, kidnap and imprisonment and starvation. Flynn couldn't find it in himself to distrust her any more, and with the distrust gone, he was reminded again that she had chosen to stay by his side when she might have got through the portal scot-free. She was entitled to behave like a woman every now and again and have a good sob.

Another time and he would even have been glad to offer his shoulder to cry on, but this was not that time. "I'm just worried about the skipper."

"I know you are." The curl of her lip shifted from wobbly to contemptuous in an instant, but then she said "ah!" and pointed the wand at the cage door. All the metal tendrils began to unravel, drawing themselves inwards like a snail withdrawing his eyes from a hostile world.

"You beauty!" Overcome with relief, Flynn caught her up and spun her in a wild jangle of bells. Kissed her on the cheek, in a moment of exhilaration and softness, enveloped in a clean scent. Her hair smelled like jasmine, and her skin like sandalwood. The slap didn't register until a moment later, but then it made him back off, raise his hands in surrender and, laughing, say, "I'm sorry. I was just happy. I didn't mean anything by it."

"Don't do that again." Her glare could have pared diamond. They stood trapped in it for what seemed a very long time, before he said again, seriously now, "You're right. I am sorry."

She shook the memory off her like a dog shaking off water, eeled out of the remaining tendrils of the cage and stood in the quiet stone room, head tilted, listening.

He picked up his helmet from the floor and slid it on, tiptoed out after her. "What?"

"Do you hear that?"

It was already so silent that he thought he could hear the slow *shhh* of the dust piling up, but at Sumala's words he half-guessed at a vanishingly faint sliding noise. He followed her, and it, as she stalked the sound, still with that graceful gait he had noticed in the meadow, still moving as though the survival of the universe turned on the perfect placing of her feet. She walked as though she was dancing.

But we've already established she's not for you. She's just made that perfectly clear. He tucked the thought away into the same mental oubliette where he'd stowed his future. Better not to think, better just to listen. Even he, with his mortal ears, had begun to guess at the sound of flowing water now, and he knew what that meant.

"Here," she said, pulling on the sculpted arm of one of the dancers carved on the wall. "I can't get it open. Can you?"

Flynn couldn't see any evidence of a door, but he took hold of the stone nevertheless and tugged with all his might. The stone ground outwards, grittily cushioned on a layer of fine sand, and a burst of colder air billowed in, set the tapestries waving on the walls, bringing their colours to light—faded madder reds and turquoise blue.

The air smelled of dragon dung, metallic sweet, and of algae and damp. The sound of the river was unmistakable now. Geoff set his feet down and brushed off his hands. Where he'd touched the carving, its layer of dust had come away. The arm showed glossy black beneath the handprint.

Returning with the room's single lantern, Sumala went ahead of him into the dark. The globe of light about her showed rough-hewn stone passages intersecting one another, steps down and up.

"It's a regular warren." Flynn felt in his pocket for his notebook and pencil, began mapping the way they had taken, all the turnings they had passed by. "Why does the queen need all of this, when everyone else in the city gets by with a single street?"

"She needs to be able to move about secretly." The lantern flickered in Sumala's hand, its flame guttering wildly. Brown misshapen shadows flitted about the walls. Before her feet lay a square of blackness, and from it the cold blast came up, setting her headdress ringing. "She can't walk down the main street without an escort of thirty-three nobles, ninety-nine knights and five hundred and twenty men at arms."

She looked back and smirked. He guessed he was forgiven.

"Also conjurers, jugglers, minstrels, fire eaters, griffons, dragonets and human slaves."

"Ah, all the pomp and ceremony." Geoff grinned back, though the words "human slaves" had not improved since he heard them last.

"Also because she fears assassination." Sumala set her foot into the square of darkness, and the light she held just touched the single step beneath her with dismal grey. "All rulers fear assassination, but some have more cause than others. At any rate, I knew the tunnels must be here. The last queen and she before her, they have all feared assassination and been unable to move freely about their realm except in secret. It is one of the ways in which power takes away our freedom."

It was an interesting thought, and had Flynn been sitting in the Rose and Crown at home he'd have been willing to debate it. Here, however, he just gestured her forward and said, "Shall we?"

At the bottom of the ladderlike steps, they came again to the slow, black river. A little jetty jutted into the water, making the river eddy just enough to give it a voice. It was the sad gurgle and sucking noise as the smooth-flowing stream curled around the pillars of this which they had heard, up in their prison. There was no boat.

Flynn contemplated going back, trying to find another route through the maze of passages, the chances of coming out in some public area where they'd be spotted and caught. "We'll have to swim."

"I can't!" Sumala dipped her toes in the water, her reflected anklet shining bright. She drew her foot back as if the water had stung her.

"God bless the RAF," said Flynn, unbuckling his life jacket. "Take all that gold off and put this on. We've only got to float downstream until we're out of the city. I'll keep hold of you and get us both to shore."

She bit her lip, tested the water again with no more enthusiasm than last time. He waited for her to suggest that they take another passage—he knew, after all, that she couldn't care less if he made his rendezvous with the skipper or not. Half an hour extra here or there was nothing to her.

But then she reached up and unpinned the crown from her head, disentangling the strings of golden bells and birds from her fine black hair. She held it in front of her as lantern light made the little ornaments seem to stir with fugitive light, and then she drew her arm back and flung it into the middle of the stream. A brief glitter showed beneath the surface as it plummeted through the first transparent layers of water, then it was gone. She followed it with the massive collar, bracelets, anklets, armlets and earrings.

Flynn understood that she had to leave them at the bottom of the river, where no one would find them. She couldn't risk having something so personal to her as her clothing found by a mage, who could use it to establish a magic link to her, influence her from afar, even kill her from afar with it.

She looked a hundred percent more naked without them all, but no smaller, no less dignified. She'd kept back a single golden chrysanthemum that lay on a slender gold chain along her parting. It troubled him to see her without the ornaments, without the glimmer that accompanied every movement. She looked suddenly too vulnerable to be traipsing around the place in nothing but a see-through skirt. "Here," he said, stripping off his overalls and offering them first. "This'll stop the straps from chafing."

She picked the coveralls up with a little smile. He hadn't said thank you for her decision to face the river for his sake. So now she didn't say thank you for the gesture of trust, just put his clothing on and followed it with the life jacket.

The river was icy cold. They broke through a skin of it at the surface and were chased down the flow by fragile sheets of ice, hair thick. Sumala lay back, eyes closed, trusting her weight to the float and her destination to Flynn. He clung on to her webbing and fended them off the walls until the entrance passed gold above them and they burst out into the gorse thicket at the base of the slope where the mound of the city rose up from its surrounding meadow.

The roots dipping down from the bank were slippery, but together they managed to cling on, pull themselves out and lie in hiding under the stems of gorse, looking out while they made sense of what they saw.

On the plain outside the city, Oonagh's bodyguard were assembling. The ground shivered with the tread of dragons, and the sky was dark with circling eagles, each with their rider in the saddle, and each trailing great nets that brushed along the ground.

As the companies of guards formed up, they would run to the nets and climb up. Then when the nets were full, the eagle would beat its wings furiously, wheel and speed away downriver, presumably to where the portal lay. Already the advance guard was nothing but specks against the hazy white sky.

About five hundred yards away, farther up the grassy slope that was the outer shell of the city, Oonagh stood and gleamed like the sun in her bronze mail. The banner that streamed out above her was worked of cloth of gold, and figured with two fighting stallions, rearing to kick out at one another, their legs intertwined. It gave Geoff pause. He looked out again at the small army that continued to draw up and depart. They looked whimsical to him, like something out of a vanished age—a medieval wall painting come to life, and the sense of wrongness twinged again in his stomach, stronger even than hunger.

"Does that look like the same army to you? I thought the one Kanath showed us was bigger and better equipped."

"Let's ask him." Sumala had plaited her wet hair and tied it off with a bit of string she found in her overall pockets. Now she nodded at where the black dragon lay next to Oonagh's nobles, in his own patch of sunshine, drowsing.

He turned his head slightly, as though he felt their gazes, and behind the long snout Flynn saw Ben, still with that crown on his forehead. He was being buckled into armour that had obviously been made for him—it fitted him like a second skin.

Flynn thought, *I should get him back, for Skip, and for Sumala*, but he couldn't see how. Besides, the priority right now was somehow to find Liadain, get her to oppose this invasion.

Concentrate on the fate of the world first and worry about everything else later.

But how to find Liadain? Would she be back at the little landing where he'd met her first, standing as a tree opposite the portal? And what could she do about this, even if they did find her? Would she care enough to oppose it, or would she just use the chance to stage a coup while Oonagh was away?

"That's right," Sumala was saying to herself. "Come to us. I know you want to."

Kanath opened his eyes and raised his jaw from the scorched grass. He swung around to watch them, and it felt as though the whole army must know they were there, lying in a spiny thicket of gorse, yellow flowers above them and oil-slick-like sewage drying on their backs. Flynn felt in waking life now the disorienting tug just beneath the belly button, the multiple viewpoints of a conversation between shared souls.

His lungs filled up with fire, warming him through, and he could hear, at a distance, the conversation on which Kanath was eavesdropping—the low-voiced and urgent conversation between Ben and Oonagh.

"Here is your sword, and your bow. You were a famous archer. It will come back to you."

Silence, and then Ben's voice, thick and muzzy sounding, as if it struggled up through layer upon layer of sleep. "Why…why should I fight for you?"

Sweet patience in the queen's voice, as like the real thing as powdered eggs. "Because I am not your enemy. I am riding to the defence of your world and your friends. Can't you trust me as you once used to?"

Poor bastard, thought Geoff, and was tempted just to snatch the boy and take them both home. Then he could step off and let the hundred years he'd traded with the old crone snap back on him all at once, leave Ben and the skipper to handle everything else. It would be a gentle way to die, surely, and overdue.

But Sumala had not let herself be distracted. He could feel her will like a golden chain fastened in the dragon's nose. Just as if he was indeed being tugged, Kanath rose, shook himself, and began to pace down the slope towards them.

"Where are you going?" Oonagh asked him, sharp behind him, and Geoff sucked in a nervous breath of oily air and almost choked on it.

Kanath gave her the dragon equivalent of a smile, his mouth gaping and flickers of purple fire running along his narrow lips. "Somewhere that will please you."

"I mean to make you my steed for the battle."

"Change your plans."

Through the dragon's colour-blind eyes, Flynn could see Oonagh pause and think. Her smell flushed rose and indigo with suspicion and possibilities.

"You could be more convincing," Flynn said, and felt amusement and contempt echoed back from the cold and alien mind.

After a final hard stare, Oonagh inclined her head. "It is a poor queen who does not know when those about her are acting out of love for her. Go then and please me, for I have always been pleased with you."

Flynn waited and watched as Oonagh and Ben turned away, and their attendants hastily saddled a smaller blue dragon, whippier and with less of an ironic glint to its eye. When the two of them had taken off, and Kanath began to wind his cumbersome girth down the limewashed side of the hill towards them, he said, "Is it me or was that a bit suspicious?"

139

Sumala shrugged a shoulder, managing to make the movement look like poetry despite the baggy blue serge of her overalls. "Does it matter? Get on. For whatever reason, he will take us to the portal. Once we're through, I will call my father, you can help your friend, you can jam the thing open so that Liadain can come through and stop her. What does it matter why he's doing what we want, as long as he is?"

The dragon rumbled in his throat and the pitch of his flames grew almost ultraviolet. They looked cool, those blackish ripples of fire along his teeth, but they dried Flynn off in a single breath and with the second singed his hair.

"Now," he said, easing gingerly past the gape of teeth, "you see why I don't understand any of you. Of course it matters *why* you do what you do. It can be the difference between innocence and guilt, murder and accident, salvation and damnation."

"That's why you are so confused all the time." Sumala set herself down in a spine ridge with a smug air, as though she'd earned the right to criticise from so long spent inside his head. As the dragon lumbered across the lawn, built up speed and launched himself in pursuit of Oonagh and her army, he felt a surge of exhilaration that said she was right. What did it matter that he didn't know who to trust? Or that he didn't know what to do for the best? He was going home, and for the moment that was enough.

Chapter Eight

Rolling his plane away from the dragon, Chris fired up the radio again. He could have cheered when the panicked voices of the two Typhoon pilots came through, high pitched and incredulous.

"...believe it either, but do you see it?"

"You mean dragons coming out of the side of the hill? Yeah, I see it. Control...we're going to have abort. There must be something dodgy in the air mix. We're both seeing things."

Craning his neck up, Chris could see both planes as arrowheads in the sky, far above him, circling. He tapped his microphone and fell back into old habits with a feeling of relief. "Typhoon pilots? Are you reading me?"

"Who the hell are you?"

Oh, poor lads, they were having a bad day. Chris dubbed the voice Laurel, and his silent partner Hardy. Laurel was a smart lad, Chris felt—he was the one who had come up with the air-mix theory to explain what they both were looking at. Chris gave him his best official tone. "This is Wing Commander Christopher Gatrell, in the Mosquito you've been following."

"The ghost Lanc?"

"That's right. Now listen to me. I need you to pass on a message to Air Vice-Marshal Henderson. Tell him from me, the invasion is started. Relay these coordinates, get him to scramble anything he can get in the air and fly it here pronto."

"You're mad!"

"Oh yes? You see what's coming out of the ground down there?"

A clearing of the throat and then a weak "I do."

"Then I'm either as mad or as sane as you are. Get the air vice-marshal and see what he says. In the meantime, I have an unarmed kite and nothing's standing between these things and the rest of the country except for you. I'd appreciate a little containment."

Hardy had caught up now. "Do you have authority to be flying that plane?"

Chris couldn't help but laugh for scorn, even though the white dragon was airborne again, circling above him, with lemon-yellow flames streaking out of the sides of its mouth and what looked like a wicked smile. "For fuck's sake, man! What kind of a pilot are you? Make a decision, damn it."

"Even if they're real," Hardy began, "there's no evidence of hostile intent. And frankly I think they're some kind of..."

Hardy had been swinging his plane around while he spoke, now he came screaming in from the right, swooping over Chris's stationary kite like a crow mobbing a blackbird. The rockets on his right wingtip all but grooved the Perspex of Chris's cockpit as he shot over at high speed and cannoned past, over the hedge, into the field of the Nine Ladies.

Right under the wings of the dragon, Hardy's small jet shrieked, steering as though he had every confidence that it really wasn't there at all.

The dragon turned its head and raked Hardy's Typhoon from nose to tail with boiling golden fire.

"Shit!"

"Control." Laurel's voice cut over him, clipped and businesslike again. "Relay that message to Air Vice-Marshal Henderson please. Hostiles on the ground and in the air at my location. Over."

"Confirm hostiles at your location, 910? Over." The controller was a woman with a precise, well-modulated voice in which every syllable conveyed her scepticism. She wasn't unprofessional enough to blurt out *you can't be serious*, but it was clear she was thinking it.

Hardy broke in. "Control, this is 231. Yes, confirm hostiles. They just got me with some sort of flamethrower. Tell the brass to scramble everything. Over."

He might not deal well with a sudden influx of dragons, but Hardy was a hell of a pilot. He flipped the Typhoon on its axis, its jets wailing needle sharp, and he was fifty feet off the ground, in danger of grazing the tops of the standing stones, coming straight at the white dragon as it flapped its heavy way up into the moonlit sky.

White wings beat like a flurry of snow against the darkness. With a burst of red fire, the Typhoon let fly one of its wingtip rockets.

It locked on and as the dragon folded its wings and dived away the slim rocket left a glowing trail as it spiralled in pursuit. Chris had a moment of fierce satisfaction—this would teach the woman with the sharp face not to mess with humankind—before the white dragon whipped itself around so fast he almost expected to hear the crack and let out a focussed white sword of plasma heat from its lips.

The rocket plunged into that laser intense burst of heat. With a blast he had to turn away from, shield his eyes to protect his night vision, it exploded short of its target and a little rain of shrapnel pattered down onto Chris's cockpit.

He pulled his binoculars out of the navigator's seat pocket and focussed on the now-gaping hole in the hillside. "Keep them busy, boys. Something else is happening over there."

Around the portal, an elvish army had emerged. There were chariots and naked spearsmen painted all over with knots and vines. There were moving trees and women with sulky faces and very red lips, armed with nothing but their overlong fingernails. There were faceless soldiers in dull grey-green armour, and some in boiled leather, whose skin was so heavily tattooed they might as well have been wearing masks. Their eyes shone strangely out of the patterns. When they closed them, the eyelids too were tattooed, and the face altogether disappeared.

Another five dragons were there, the largest an equal of the white dragon, the smallest closer to the size of a T-Rex. A clear liquid dripped from its fangs and smoked on the grass, leaving perfect round burns.

All of them had begun to form themselves into rough companies and to move out, drawing away from the portal, but had been frozen in place, looking up, with dismay, at the two jets unexpectedly there to meet them.

Now, however, the soil of the hill was moving again, pattering down from the portal to pool around the stones. The side of the slope bulged out and with a movement that looked like a landslide, an eagle's beak broke the surface. It gave a harsh cry and wriggled itself free as if it were hatching out of the ground. But there was a warrior on its back and a dozen others beneath it, holding tight to a net it was grasping in its talons. As soon as their feet hit the earth, the net was dropped and they ran out, making way for the others who followed.

The army already in occupation turned, raising their shields. If he focussed as far as the binoculars would go, Chris could see the thunderstruck look on their faces and tell that they hadn't been expecting this at all.

Who was who? He had no idea, but when the eagles dropped their load and flew up to engage the white dragon in combat, he could have cheered regardless.

A knight came through on horseback, his banner of cloth of gold. Chris recognised the device, the rearing horses which had run in a band around that circlet Ben had been wearing, and his heart hit him in the throat and stopped him breathing. *They wouldn't, would they? They wouldn't let him through? Bring him with them?*

Skirmishes had started up all about the bottom of the mound as impatient warriors of the horse army engaged the white army's rearguard. In the air the other five dragons soared up to join their leader, and together they grappled and burned the eagles.

The Typhoons had disengaged, were circling again, at a loss. "Come in, Mosquito? Which side are we on? Over."

"Neither. Both are hostile. Repeat, both are hostile. I..."

A blue snout poked its way out from beneath the hill. With a snakelike squirm, another wyrm was through, shaking the fine soil off itself. Earth fell away as though it was metal repelled by a magnet, leaving the riders pristine.

Chris forgot what he had been going to say, slid back his chair, had put down the radio headset before his brain caught up with him and he snatched it up again, pressed it to his cheek. "Listen, boys, I have a rescue mission to go on. There's a civilian down there being held captive. I'm going to go, infiltrate, try and get him out, okay? Cover me? Over."

145

"This whole fucking thing is mad." Hardy's voice, sharper now and focussed. "And they can't get hold of Henderson. He's up to something hush-hush and isn't answering his mobile. We've asked for confirming flights from London, but the Met boys are quibbling over the fucking volcanic ash. And bloody hell, if we're just going insane…"

"He means yes, Wingco. Go, we'll cover you. Over."

Chris landed on the tarmac of the deserted road, the noise of the battles covering his footsteps. A little way down the road, a stile cut through the hawthorn hedge. The path there approached the hill from the north—keeping the bulk of it between him and the two confused armies. Crouched down and in his dark clothes, he thought with luck he could get there with no one seeing him. Coming back again with Ben… Well, he'd cross that bridge when he came to it.

He reached the hill without difficulties. The sentries on top of it were fighting each other. Pulling his hood farther down, he began to edge around the fosse at the base of the hill, keeping to the patches of long grass, the rhododendrons and gorse.

He was breathing hard, winded with haste and nerves, as he rounded the final shoulder and saw the ribbon of blue dragon still with its tail embedded in the mound. There was another queen atop it, this one in scale armour, with no helmet, her white hair floating like cobweb about a face so midnight black he could see nothing of it in the dark but the bright blue eyes.

Ben sat behind her. There had been seven eagles, now their corpses lay on the field and burned with a crackle of fat. In their corpse light, and the light of the jewel on Ben's forehead, Chris could see the blank bemusement on Ben's face, and it sickened him. That wasn't staying voluntarily, it was being drugged and chained. It would have to stop.

Under the Hill: Dogfighters

The horse queen yelled a command, her piercing voice like a needle through Chris's eye. It wasn't a big army she had—little more than a bodyguard. At her words they drew up in a circle around her, as if to begin the battle with a last stand. Certainly the larger white army lapped them round on every side, facing inwards now. There was an exchange of formal taunts and posturing that reminded him of rival gangs of football hooligans on a match night after the pubs were closed.

While they were focussed on each other, Chris edged along the hill until he was close enough to reach up and grab Ben's ankle. He was conscious, with a sickening intensity, of the heat of the dragon's flank behind which he sheltered, how easy it would be for the massive thing to shrug him into the side of the hill and squash until he was pulp.

Over to starboard one of the Typhoons dispatched another rocket, caught a dragon on the ground. There was a *whoomph* of explosion, a mushroom cloud of orange gas and blast front of heat. Everyone looked, and Chris grabbed Ben and pulled with all his might.

Ben swayed in his seat, caught drunkenly at the spine ridge of the dragon but couldn't seem to close his fingers. As Chris pulled again, he came sliding, reeling off, his arms windmilling, with a great shout of shock.

He landed in a sprawl. Chris tried to catch him but only ended up half-pinned beneath Ben's dead weight, as the queen turned and fixed him with a gaze as sharp as broken glass.

Chris wrenched his face away from the glare, twisted out from beneath Ben and looked down at him. He lay inert and absent, a shell of himself, and Chris shook him hard, wanting the man he knew back more than anything he'd ever wanted in his life. "Wake up! Ben! Wake up!"

The queen laughed, took the spear from its rest on the side of her saddle and with a move so fast Chris could not even see it, she pressed its tip to his back. It was like sticking his finger in a light socket. Everything in him clenched painfully and stopped, his heart felt iced in place, his muscles petrified. An intolerable strangeness itched its way through all his cells, came out of his mouth in a strangled whine.

He'd just had a mad and poetic idea, didn't know if it would work but it was bloody well worth a try. Barely able to work his limbs, he managed to bring his knee up in a staccato, broken-clockwork movement, and pin Ben's hip to the ground.

The semi-paralysis left a terrified, metallic aftertaste in his mouth as his heart stuttered into life again. His first breath felt like the touch of a fork to a bad filling. "I..." He coughed, wishing he could wipe his streaming eyes. The ballad of Tam Lin did not mention the faithful rescuer having to sniff back snot as she held tight to her abducted lover. Perhaps that detail had been edited out by the minstrels over the years.

"There are rules about this," he said. "I want him back. You know how this works."

Flinging a long leg over the saddle, the queen slid down, landing with the kind of grace and elegance that could have inspired a whole verse. There were white triskeles that glowed like pearl painted on her blue-black face, and she looked as if she had all the time in the world. Regal, amused, perhaps even a little bit charmed. "You're no Jenny Fair."

Chris didn't dare shrug, made do with raising his eyebrows, while Ben came alive beneath him—tried to simultaneously knee him and prize his grip undone. "Times change. But it's the same thing underneath."

"True love?" she mocked, putting the heel of her mailed boot over his hand and pressing down. He yelped and pulled it away, keeping hold with the other, while he brought his bruised fingers back and tangled them in Ben's over-embroidered collar.

"Well let's see."

Chris had the thought only just in time. He shifted his grip to the skin of Ben's flailing wrist, getting hit in the nose for the trouble. The young man's left elbow cracked him in the jaw, but it had been worth it, as the collar he'd been gripping only a moment ago turned to mist and flowed out between his fingers.

Ben growled deep in his throat, the sound growing hoarser, deeper, wilder, as the skin beneath Chris's fingers shifted into fur, the teeth by his cheek lengthened and the blank, ferocious eyes turned tawny. He found himself trying to hold down a lion by its front legs, ducked his head at the last moment and twisted so that its powerful jaw closed on his shoulder, the flesh-ripping teeth locked in the muscle.

Fuck! Oh, you, goddamn fucking shit! Pain like acid tore through his veins, stopped his heart again, but he gritted his teeth, choked back the automatic recoil and held on, nothing but sheer willpower keeping his hands closed, though the nerves in both arms felt shredded and incapable, misfiring in panic and agony.

When he could control his fingers again he let go with the right hand, grabbed the lion by its muzzle, two fingers in its nostrils, his grip sliding in the mess of saliva and blood. He clamped down hard and felt it shift again, the teeth withdrawing from his flesh more painfully than they went in.

The flesh under his fingers had begun to liquefy, his hand sunk in. As it did, he realised the blood on it had disappeared. His shoulder still throbbed and burned as if wounded, but when he turned to look, the material of his shirt was undamaged, the skin beneath untouched. He flexed his fingers to be sure he still could and gasped in a shaky breath of relief. *Illusion. Thank God!*

Yes, thank God, because the form beneath him had now reshaped itself into something he couldn't at first understand. The head had flattened but expanded outwards into a wet, gelatinous mess stained flamingo pink. There was something a little harder in the body that rolled with a damp suggestion of gristle under his knees, and the arms in his grasp had become long, beautiful, slippery streamers.

All of this he saw in a moment's burst of sight, photographic in its brevity, but that was the last thing he saw before the agony of the sting hit him and turned his brain and viscera to boiling lead. The pain ate him out from inside. He'd never felt anything like it—scarcely felt it now, it was too huge to comprehend, too raw to process. He couldn't think, breathe, move or weep, but the long ribbons of the creature's arms were slippery in his hands, pulling away from him.

Somewhere in the back of his skull that he hadn't visited since the crash, was a little reservoir of calm. In there the part of himself that was greater than the animal, separate from the flesh, still watched and thought. *It's a man-of-war jellyfish*, it told him. *You think you're paralysed, but you're not, because it's an illusion. Move now. Hold on!* But he couldn't move and he couldn't hold on. He could feel it drawing away and could not force his hands to close on the stinging spines, to grip hard enough to make this worse.

You'll lose him.

Scarcely managing to breathe, he tipped himself forward until gravity could take him farther, make him fall face first into the pulsing bell of the creature. There was no more pain that he could take—he'd reached overload—so opening his mouth and biting down, holding on tight with his teeth, didn't do more than make him feel as if the inside of his mouth had been scoured off with pumice. He thought he heard the queen laugh again, behind him, and he was surprised, because he'd forgotten she existed.

The burning in his veins changed. He could feel the shape begin to writhe into something new, and wanted to weep. How long? How long was he supposed to keep this up? Forever? How many shapes did they expect him to go through? But the despair eased as his paralysis ebbed away with the disappearing man-of-war. Holding on tight with one hand and mouth, Chris reached farther up, trying to get at that circlet on Ben's head so that he could yank it off.

But the agony in his hands had returned. He looked down, did a double take, saw his right hand clamped about a steering yoke. The body beneath him had become a seat, a bank of dials, glowing phosphorescent beneath the ruby red light that shone into the cockpit. *Oh God*, Chris thought, feeling his stomach drop and cold sweat break out down his spine. *This isn't playing fair.* He could already smell the stench of combusted wool, the sticky sweet, horrifyingly mouthwatering smell of roasted airman.

This isn't...this isn't fair. The steering yoke of the plane was now red hot, he could see his own hands shrivel and smoke, watch the skin burst and the blood underneath boil. Flames raged from all four engines and the rush of falling flattened him to his seat, the ground spinning and hurtling towards him. He knew it wasn't real, but he couldn't make that knowledge connect with the overwhelming swell of loss and grief and panic. *I can't do this again. Don't make me do this again. Please God!*

How to even work out where Ben's head was in this scenario? Chris's fingers were nothing more than charred bones now, but he locked his elbow around the yoke, and with the club of his other arm flailed at the cockpit above, half hoping to knock the circlet off, half madly intent on breaking the Perspex so that he could fall out of this hell-kite, fall through clean sky and break himself painlessly, instantly on the ground beneath.

As he flailed, his foot impacted with something soft. He looked down and saw he'd just kicked through the crisped and brittle bones of Archie's head, and his boot was embedded in the skull. He heard a little high-pitched whine come out of his mouth, and then he was letting go of the already shifting yoke, curling up, weeping salty tears on his quickly healing hands. No. He couldn't do it any more. He couldn't—there just was a limit beyond which a man couldn't go, and he'd reached it, and if there was a God up there, then thank God he was a forgiving one because Chris simply couldn't measure up. He'd tried, but he couldn't.

"Chris?" Someone was shaking him. He hardly noticed at first, overloaded with sensation and grief, but it went on, gentle shaking, and Ben's voice saying urgently, "Chris? Come on! We're still in a war zone, wake up!"

Archie had done that once. That time when they'd lost two engines and been coned in that spotlight, and he'd had to throw the great weight of the plane through acrobatics she hadn't been designed for for half an hour. When he'd been so weary afterwards he'd tried to jump, Archie had stopped him with a punch to the jaw. Best bloody friend a man could have.

"Chris!"

There was a hand beneath his shoulder, pulling him. He made a heroic effort to pull himself together, sniffed and rubbed his cuff over his eyes. He'd been a boy fresh out of school in those days and had some excuse. Now, he should know better.

He tried to sit up, but his right arm seemed stuck. When he looked down, he found that *Ben* was holding *him* around the wrist. Wiping his face again, he got his feet under him and lurched up to standing, looked at Ben with incredulity, with a feeling that he'd fallen down the rabbit hole, left sense and reason behind. Ben's eyes were clear, the wrinkles of a smile about them, full of intelligence and a fine new self-confidence Chris hadn't seen before.

He didn't understand. "But I failed."

Ben exchanged his grip on Chris's wrist for a supportive arm around his shoulders, and showed him the circlet that he held in his other hand. "You knocked it off," he said. "At the end there. Accidentally, maybe, I don't know. But you knocked it off, and after that I was able to hold on to you."

"S-so it worked?" Chris had been so crushed, so defeated, the sudden reversal gave him seasickness. His mouth watered with nausea.

"Well..." Ben laughed, and the high-pitched sound proclaimed bad news. "Yes, it worked. And thank you." He gestured at the darkness that surrounded them, a darkness filled with the plumes of dragonfire, the pale glimmer of elvish armour. "But we're still in the middle of a war."

Chris looked for the queen, found her atop her dragon, looking out with a grim expression, her lips a thin blue line. She caught him watching and gave him a distracted salute, an ironic mimicry of his RAF days. "The rules say nothing about who lets go first," she said. "But if ever I needed a champion—if ever I needed your aid, it is now."

Chris took a few deep breaths, trying to still the trembling in his legs, the muscle memory of all that pain. "You expect me to *help you*? After you put me through all that?"

He turned his back and walked away, scrambling up the side of the hill, but all that did was to give him a better view of the battle, and she was right. The eagles had proved no match for the white army's dragons. This horse queen's small force were surrounded by the larger, better drilled and better armed forces of the white queen.

Wheels in his head turned reluctantly, almost despite him. Wasn't it after all the woman on the white dragon—the white queen—who had come through first, who had only been stopped from marching her forces to the nearest town by the timely intervention of two chance-met Typhoon pilots? And didn't that make hers the invasion force, and this woman's intervention something in the nature of a counterstrike?

"It's true." Ben threw the circlet on the ground, where it lay like an ancient treasure dug from a barrow mound. He scrambled up the bank beside Chris, grabbed his arm again, as if despite his no-nonsense speech he could not quite stop himself from touching. "Liadain is the aggressor here—that's the one on the white dragon. Oonagh's trying to stop her."

"Normally I'd believe you implicitly, but that thing..." An arrow hit the ground by Chris's foot and two others hummed past him with a sound like swan wings.

He jumped back down into the shelter of the fosse and kicked mud over the mercury shimmer of the crown's central diamond. *A star on his forehead, eh?* That explained why Tam Lin had not tried to get away on his own before his sweetheart could rescue him.

Ben followed, something about his face older, grimmer than it had been. "She didn't need to do that. I would have helped her anyway. I suppose she just needed to be sure." He took a quick breath. "Listen. I am a reincarnation of someone called Karshni. Their world is dying. Oonagh has this plan to build ships to take them to another world, but she needs Karshni's father's help to do it and he won't give it. She thought I could persuade him, that's why she needed me.

"But Liadain is a traditionalist—she doesn't believe in spaceships and new worlds, she wants to take back the world that humans drove her people from in prehistory. She wants to take our world. Oonagh came to stop her."

One of the white queen's dragons was headed their way, trying to outfly one of the Typhoons. A second dragon rose up stealthily as the plane passed, folded its wings like a hawk and plummeted out of the moonlight, a thousand tonnes of beast impacting with the smaller, faster dart of the jet.

Built for agility and speed, the plane was not designed to be rammed midair, nor equipped to be torn at by meter-long, diamond-tipped claws. There was a roar as the dragon aimed point-blank flame at the plane held like a toy in its claw. All the incendiaries and missiles left on the airframe exploded at once. Chris heard the punch and hiss of an ejector seat and was just feeling good about the white parachute spreading in the steel-grey moonlit sky when the dragon shook off the flaming mess of aircraft from its paw and turned to incinerate the silk as it slowly floated down.

He couldn't possibly have heard the thud of the pilot striking the ground at hundreds of miles an hour over the battle cries, but imagination provided it nonetheless.

"I cannot afford for my political enemies to gain a victory here," Oonagh had followed them. Her chilly observation cut calmly through Chris's grief. "Not when many of my people would be happy to take the easier option and follow her to your world. That way proved disastrous the last time, and I am not willing to take the risk again. My strategy was to avoid this, to avoid war. That's where you come in. You and your crew. You were to prevent this happening."

"You might have told us. You might have asked," Chris said, sullen, because he had treasured his grievances over the past fifteen years. He didn't want to think that she might just have been acting for the best. "It didn't occur to you to just be honest with us both? And what about Red? Archie? They were just collateral damage? Friendly fire?"

The elf woman looked at him, her head on one side and her brows twisted. "I don't understand what you're asking."

He had to laugh. It was that or cry again, and he'd done enough of that for one night. "Of course you don't. Very well. For the sake of the world, count me in. I don't know what I can do, but you've got me. You're fucking lucky I don't bear a grudge."

He looked out. It didn't take the extra rise of the hill to see the enemy now. Oonagh's forces had thinned and drawn back, there were barely three ranks of warriors between her and the front line of the enemy troops. Her lips moved as she directed the commanders by her thought, but it was growing close enough that she could as well have shouted.

The arrows had been spent and it was hand-to-hand work out there. Chris watched as a white rush of fog on his left turned into one of the taloned women, who reached out a languid arm to a knight in full armour, absorbing every blow of his sword with nothing more than a slow seep of black blood. She snapped his neck with one hand and then lowered her face to his throat and ripped it out with her perfect white teeth.

"Shit! Ben, I'm going to have to..." He turned back, found Ben offering Oonagh a small pouch of dirt.

"I should contact my father," Ben was saying. "Does anyone here have water?"

"Where did you get this?" Oonagh asked, turning the thing over in her palms as if it were a small bird—as if she feared to frighten it. "A queen made this, but it has a price that few would be willing to pay. Oh, this explains much. Yes, talk to him. Tell him... Tell him that I have news he needs to hear."

"He's going to be pissed at you."

"I am willing to take that chance."

"Right then," Chris said, again with a feeling of ill-use. So that rescue had been completely pointless, had it? Damn it all, if he survived this, he was going to have a lovely long sulk afterwards. "I'll just go then, shall I?"

Keeping low, dodging from place to place and threading through the gaps between combatants, his only defence a quick flinch away and legging it fast, Chris made his way back to the hedge.

Over the stile, he dropped onto the tarmac of another world. That was how it felt. If he looked back, it was to see a battlefield like something out of myth, if forwards, it was a seldom-used country road, with its white lines recently repainted, and a single orange streetlamp.

This night's work would take a lot of reflection to get straight in his head, but he didn't have time for introspection now. He dashed back to his Mosquito, took off and surveyed the damage in the air. Dragons fought around him, filling the slatey sky with multicoloured plumes of flame. Four of them boxed in the second Typhoon, were trying to get him to hold position enough to be caught in the same manoeuvre that had finished the first. There was no sign of any RAF reinforcements.

"You still there, boys?" Chris whispered as he circled above the action, wondering what he could do without ordnance, and the hiss of static in his ears became the deeper, infinite echoey hiss of the afterlife.

"Still here, Skipper." The voice brought back the moment he'd broken down there. It wasn't fair, was it, that you could

157

decide you couldn't take any more, and the world would just go ahead and give you more regardless.

"I'm sorry, Archie. All of you. It was my job to bring you home... I'm sorry."

From under his feet, Archie said, "Oh, can it," just as Red remarked, "Less chitchat, we've got work to do," and he found himself surrounded by ghostly laughter.

He joined in because apart from the fact that he was alive and they weren't, this was almost exactly like old times. "All right then, skipper to gunners, can you give me weapons?"

A chorus of two "Hell, yes!" and one "Affirmative" answered him. "What d'you think we're here for, Skip?" said Red, their enthusiasm palpable. Outside the cockpit, the moon shone once more on the pale, ethereal fuselage of a phantom Lancaster, enveloping the real plane and subsuming it.

Through the radio, Chris could hear the whining of servos as the gunners made sure their turrets moved smoothly, and he was grinning as he swung her about, found the white dragon, starlit in the leaden sky. High above the action, she observed and controlled her forces like a careful general, far away from danger herself.

Not far enough.

"Right you are, chaps. Target is the big white bastard. I'll get you close, you do the rest."

Chris leaned back on the yoke, slicing upwards, grabbing altitude, with the engines thundering and throbbing and every rivet rattling in its socket. Painted black against a black sky, the Lanc was nothing more than an onrushing wave of sound. Liadain, intent on the fight below, did not spot them swinging around behind her until the front and mid-upper gunners opened fire, bullets white as vapour from the guns and the muzzle flame a pale cold blue.

Under the Hill: Dogfighters

Occe's guns blazed, tearing into a wing. A pattern of dark holes opened in the membrane, and white blood fell like snow from where the shots had lodged in the long bones.

The creature screamed, its injured wing flapping loose and fast. It began to lose height. But as Chris roared past so that Red, in the tail gun, could take his shots, it craned its neck hard and an inferno of flame roared from its jaws, enveloping the tailplane and the rear turret. Chris pictured the Perspex melting, all the bullets on their belt bursting... Too many rear gunners he'd known had had to be washed out of their cockpits with a hose—there being nothing solid left.

Then Red gave a whoop of laughter, and peppered the dragon's nose with bullets, chipping teeth. "I'm dead already, sucker! Can't touch me now!"

This was not entirely true. The steering felt strange, and if Chris twisted round to look he could see, beneath the sooty cloak of Lancaster, a suggestion of red light where the Mosquito's rudder should be. "We're on fire!"

He disengaged, leaving the white dragon to flap itself pathetically to the ground, sit there hunched and insulted as a wet cat, the woman on its back raising her fist in defiance at him.

The moonlight was scattered over Bakewell by long lines of mare's-tail clouds, and along the railway cumulus had begun to pile up, the night's clear cold air turning damp. Chris took the Mosquito into the cloudbank, circled in there until the glow on the tail had gone down. The rudder felt loose beneath his feet, but he still had control. Some of it must be left, at least.

When he burst back out into clear skies his long-distance view of the battlefield looked like a fireworks display. There was even a red glow on the ground where another dragon had finally succumbed to the Tornado's missiles. The radio crackled in his

159

ear. "Control, I'm serious, we need those reinforcements. I'm running out of ammo and we have one man down. What the hell are you doing back there?"

Chris couldn't hear the reply, but the pilot's "Shit, what's *that!*" came through loud and clear. He came down to one hundred feet, scoured the ground, looking for whatever had prompted the response, and saw the whole side of the hill bulge out. Something flew through. It was hard to see in the dark. He caught glimmers from claws sheathed in diamonds, a flicker of aquamarine fire along a long jaw, and eyes, molten gold as the eyes of a toad.

The hill closed up behind it. It was already in flight, climbing with powerful wing beats. Looking down, it hadn't seen him. The very tip of one great wing snapped up and punched the Lanc in the bomb bay, and as he hauled back on the stick, tearing the plane up and to the side, shearing away from it, he saw two small figures clinging to its back, their faces upraised to gawp at him, mouths open.

He gained altitude, looped the tightest turn he could manage, the skin pulling away from his cheeks with the g-force, intended to skim straight back over the creature's head, see if he had ghost bombs in the bay. A 500-pound incendiary, dropped through its spine, should give even this massive brute some trouble.

The second pass gave him the chance to study the figures on its back. Gave him the chance to do a double take, check three, four times more. A dark-haired girl in a pair of RAF coveralls and...

Good God, it wasn't, was it? Couldn't be Geoff, still in the outfit he'd worn seventy years ago, curls pressed flat by his flying helmet, wiping the soil off his goggles as the dragon passed beneath the Mossie and looked up as if it knew it had shivered his world to the roots.

"Skipper to bomb aimer, tell me that's not Flynn?"

"Bomb aimer here. Looks like our navigator to me, sir."

He'd breathed in something fizzy, it could be the only explanation for the effervescence he could feel in his chest or the fact that something was making it hard to get out any words. "Fantastic! Let's give him covering support, yes?"

But Geoff and the girl had got their bearings now, taken a slow sweep over the battle and lined up on Oonagh. They were flying straight at her. She'd noticed, launched her own mount into the sky. Whip thin, it looked by comparison, a long slender lizard by the side of the black dragon's bulk. It flamed a green burst of territorial fire, but it was like watching a lion cub swipe at the nose of the pride's king—childish, doomed.

Damn! It didn't occur for a moment to Chris that Geoff might be in Liadain's pay. Lied to, he thought. Misled. He switched on the radio, thought of telling the remaining Typhoon pilot to defend the queen—thought again, because that would mean sending a barrage of missiles Geoff's way.

He peeled off, gave the engines all the power he had available and got enough of a head start so that he could loop behind the hill and charge in from the opposite direction, flying straight at the black dragon's nose. Unless one of them lost their nerve soon, they would collide just above Oonagh's head, with unimaginable damage to them both.

"Skipper to wireless operator. Flynn's wearing his helmet, can you patch him into the intercom?"

"It's an intercom, Skip. He's not exactly 'in'."

"Don't give me that crap, Tolly. I'm flying a ghost kite above a portal between worlds I opened by the power of prayer. Don't expect me to play by the laws of physics now. Just do it!"

They were coming in fast, Chris's biceps twinged with the need to pull up, pull up right now and avoid the collision. He could hear Tolly muttering about wires in his left ear, hear the deep *whuum, whuum* of four well-adjusted engines and the shriller tone of the two Mosquito props. Cold sweat gathered under his collar and made the headset chafe against his cheek where the old scar lay silver from one too many wartime blisters. He could see the faces of the dragon riders, the little golden ornament the woman wore in her hair, the look of utter bemusement on Geoff's face, familiar to Chris as his own.

"Five seconds. You're cutting it fine!"

"Ah! Got it! There you..."

There was the sharp snap of a connection in his right earphone. "Flynn? Flynn, pull up!"

"Skipper?"

Chris almost stood in his seat, elbows through the yoke, pulling it back with all the strength in his back and his legs. At the same time, the black dragon folded its wings and dropped sixty feet. It levelled out, scarcely higher than a man's upraised arm, turned on a wingtip, and with its head down like a man labouring to peddle a bicycle up a hill, it worked to regain the height it had lost. Even so, the ghost tailplane of the Lanc grazed the end of the dragon's floating tail, slithering along the barb with a metallic screech.

"Skipper? Skip, is that you? What the hell? I nearly had her."

"You're going for the wrong one, sunshine. It's the one on the white dragon you want to take out. Liadain, she's the genius who cooked up the idea to invade earth."

"She...told me..." Flynn's voice had none of the white noise to it, the scratchy hollow sound of the other boys. But it did sound painfully identical to how it had sounded back in the days of Chris's vanished youth. That shouldn't hurt so much.

"Geoff? It's great to hear your voice again."

"Yeah. Yeah, I could say the same, Skip. I really could."

Chris pulled out of his ascent and levelled off, tried to rub off his grin. What he saw managed it far more successfully than he desired. The Typhoon was peeling away, returning to base with all its ammunition spent. Deprived of that target, Liadain's dragons had seen Oonagh's weakness and were mustering to attack. There were five of them left, and they had joined one another in a loose formation directly above the single stone on top of the hill. They parted like a flower opening, one attacking Oonagh from the front, one from the back and one each side.

The final, largest one dived directly for Geoff, claws outstretched to pluck him from his dragon's back. At the same time something hit Chris's kite amidships, sailing straight through the Lanc and smashing into the Mosquito beneath, splintering the wood, leaving a hole the size of his head. The missile rolled about the fuselage behind him, a block of stone, roughly shaped into a circle. Someone down below had had time to fit together a trebuchet and had shattered one of the standing stones to turn into shot.

Chris ignored the howling wind that was now whipping around the compartment, pulled down his goggles to protect his eyes and moved to intercept Geoff's attacker. It was another white dragon. A beautiful thing, the way its scales were patterned with what looked like lotus flowers in yellow. It shone in the moonlight as if it were hammered out of silver and gold, but Chris was much more concerned about the way it had managed to get one long claw embedded in the black dragon's wing joint, was reaching its swan neck down to let loose a bolt of flame straight in Geoff's face. Geoff, God bless him, was trying to hold the jaws away from himself and buckling flat under the strain.

"Skipper to gunners, give it every damn thing you've got."

He'd never flown the Lanc as a gun platform, always used his gunners as lookouts only unless something was directly attacking *them*. This was his first experience with what the Fighter Boys called "the kill". It was fucking *awesome* to dive on an enemy with the gun turrets blazing, to see the shots go home, and put out the dragon's fire with a burst to the throat. Red's work, that. It left Geoff nothing to do but stand up, kick the great claw unclenched and lever the body over the side. He let it fall like a stone on one of the groves of moving trees, shattering them.

"Thanks, Skipper!"

"Don't mention it, Navigator, but you can do me a favour and take out that bloody trebuchet, would you?"

"I'm on it."

Chris wanted to laugh for the glory of it, right until he had circled round again and could see how hopelessly outnumbered Oonagh was. Her forces were now limited to her bodyguard, drawn up tight around her, an elf like a walking flame trying to take down the enemy dragons with a bow.

Elsewhere on the field, Liadain's scattered army were reforming into companies. Some, closest to the road, had begun to send out scouts, scoping out how to get to the nearest town. He didn't want to think about what would happen when peaceful, sleeping Bakewell was invaded by vampires and monstrous trees, and axe-wielding eldritch warriors who regarded humanity as their ancient usurpers.

There was a grey cast to the sky in the east, and still no reinforcements.

Chapter Nine

Chris made another roaring pass of the battlefield and lined up on the knot of dragons that was all he could see of Oonagh. The occasional flash of bronze said she was still fighting in there, her own dragon clawing at the foremost of its attackers, a ball of fire hanging between them as both exhaled at once. The blue dragon's throat had expanded and throbbed as it drew in breath and flamed at the same time.

Ben was in that knot too, balancing on the blue dragon's flailing tail, defending himself unexpectedly well with a bow and arrows. Two of Liadain's wyrms were flapping about him, angling for a clear shot. Every time one opened its mouth, he would loose an arrow into its throat, and it would have to pause, scrub at its nose with its claws, cough up soot and melted arrowhead before it could try again.

Liadain had remounted herself on a smaller green dragon and now fought Oonagh face to face, Oonagh with her spear and Liadain with a trident, whose hollowed glass tips oozed with white liquid, that looked very much like the venom that dripped from her mount's teeth.

The fourth enemy dragon had been sent tumbling by a claw strike from Oonagh's mount, now it gathered itself together and stormed back in with a side attack. Its neck ruff and spine ridges stood out as it breathed in, and Chris could picture the explosion of fire that would hit both Ben and the queen in the side, nothing they could do about it without taking their attention disastrously away from the enemies they were already fighting.

"Okay, that one, and right now," he said, banking into another low rake across the battlefield, below the knot of skirmishing dragons, so that Occe in the mid-upper turret could get in on the action too. They flew directly under the belly of the yellow beast, emptied their magazines into the hollows beneath its legs, and the long, smooth scales shattered at the impact of the ghostly iron.

Chris didn't ask how it worked. He was too busy evading a dozen tonnes of unexpectedly plummeting dragon. It clipped him as it fell, sending the plane into a spin he really didn't have the height to risk. Body working on instinct, he fought the kite level again, found himself ten metres above the ground, his wingtip almost touching it as he turned onto one side to fly between two of the moving trees.

They gouged one of the standing stones from its socket, split it between them and hurled the pieces at him as he all but shook the crate apart trying to claw back altitude.

By the time Chris had the plane under control, turned for another sweep, Ben had run out of arrows. His last shot blinded one of the dragons he was fighting. He had taken out its other eye earlier, and now thin, orange blood trickled from both sockets out of which the arrows' fletching still poked. The dragon broke off the fight and dropped to lie writhing and hissing on the ground.

The other, Ben was only just managing to keep away by jabbing it in the nostrils and mouth with the spike on the end of his bow. Obviously not a particularly intelligent creature, it had not yet realised that it could back away and incinerate him from a safer distance.

Oonagh's mount was moving sluggishly, beginning to spiral downwards. In the back of its neck, two wounds bled slowly, and there was something of the drugged sleep in the way its head hung and its claws twitched. On its neck, Oonagh also bled, her bare right arm marked with a long white scar. She had caught the trident on the crossbar of her spear—designed in ancient days to stop the charge of an angry boar—and she was trying to unseat Liadain, twisting and pushing hard.

But it was clear that the venom was at work in her too. As he watched, Chris saw her knees buckle, watched her land heavily in the saddle and take a hand away from the spear to steady herself. At once, Liadain pressed her attack, twisted the trident and wrenched the weapon out of Oonagh's hand. Oonagh flailed after it as it dropped, slid against the dragon's smooth scales. Liadain drew back the trident, thrust forward, but Oonagh was still sliding sideways, the prongs of the trident passed over her head as she reached out her hands, and Geoff, standing up on the black dragon's back, passed beneath and caught her before she fell and smashed herself on the rocks below.

That dilemma solved, Chris swooped beneath the blue dragon's drooping tail, took out the beast that was attacking Ben.

Ben looked up as he passed, his face sweaty and alight with exhilaration and laughter. He gave a little salute, and Chris returned it, the life-and-death split-second quality of the exchange giving it a blaze of intensity, like a flashgun going off. He had afterimages of Ben's smile on the back of his eyes for long moments while Ben leapt down to the ground searching for spare arrows, and Chris banked again and came back for another pass.

He'd thought that had all gone quite well until he turned and saw that Oonagh's army had retreated all the way to the portal. There were scarcely a hundred of them left, holding open the way home for themselves and their queen should she decide on a retreat. If anything, Liadain's forces seemed to have grown.

Chris thought he had imagined that part, until he recognised amongst them some of Oonagh's troops who had been killed by the vampires. They now marched on the other side, their backbones showing through their ripped open throats. Revenants, with swords.

Liadain herself had also broken off for a moment to survey the scene. Now she floated alone over the battlefield, white and silver on her verdant steed, and laughed. "This is our day. The day when the throne passes back to the ancient blood from which you stole it. Go back to your ice-clad fjords, Ylfe, tell them of your deeds while I am reminding these creatures of meat that they once lived in terror of the Sidhe."

Okay, thought Chris, *taking out the leader was a good plan at the start, and right now it's all there is left that might work.* "Skipper to gunners, have we got ammo to spare for this one?"

Red gave a sucking sound between his teeth. "It's getting low, Skip. But let's give it a shot regardless. Is she the one that did this to us? The fireball? The burning? If so, shooting her down is what we're here to do."

He did, God help him, think of lying. It would have been so easy to say yes. A queen of Faerie had killed them, and this was a queen of Faerie. But he wasn't going to spend what might be his last moments on earth lying to his crew. Some loyalties, you simply couldn't betray, no matter what.

"Boys, I won't lie to you. The one that shot us down—killed you and messed up my life and Flynn's? That's the one we're fighting for. The one Flynn just saved."

Silence, and the noise of the engines muted. He wondered why for a moment, until a glance outside the cockpit showed only the two props of the Mosquito band-sawing the air by his head. The static in his ears was the mundane hiss of an untuned channel. He didn't close his eyes or put his head in his hands, but if he had not been flying, he would have. The crumpled sensation in the belly was the same.

He thought of Grace, suddenly, sitting in her church and rethinking her principles on the side of loving-kindness. He'd thought it should have been an easy choice for her, realised now it was more of a request to turn the world inside out and reshape everything she had ever known to take in a God more terribly, more super-humanly good than human nature found easy to support. Same thing here—he knew the right thing to do. He was damn sure the boys knew it too, but God it was hard! Too bloody much to ask.

But it was being asked nevertheless, and that being so, it was his job as skipper to get them safely through it.

"Listen, boys," he urged, not knowing if they were even there to hear, "maybe vengeance isn't what you're here for at all. 'Vengeance is mine, saith the Lord' am I right? That's His job. Maybe your job is to be the better man? To do the decent thing? Maybe you've been kept back so you get the chance to forgive her. What d'you think?"

He wished hard for Grace, right now. What would she say? She always knew the right thing to say. Picturing her, the way she dealt with things, he remembered that she didn't bring theology into it much, always brought it down to the here and now, to the personal. And that was the part he hated doing himself—exposing the inner man with all his vulnerabilities to the light.

He swallowed, followed her example—for the boys—and the words came by themselves, unexpected, even shameful in their intensity.

"From what I guess, you're in the anteroom of Heaven or Hell, where you are now. I don't want to see you make the wrong choice, Tolly, Archie, Red. If you're going to damn yourselves, out of fucking spite, count me out of it, okay? That's not the boys I knew. That's not my brothers in arms. Don't make me remember you badly. Don't disappoint me, okay? You'll break my bloody heart."

"You're a goddammned sap, Skipper." It was the hand that came back first, the cold fingers linked through his on the throttles, and then the faint glimmer of a shape in the flight engineer's seat. The accent was Hank's drawl, slow and steady and amused. "But I guess you're right. If we'd done what we felt like come wartime, I wouldn't never have left home. We're here to do what's the right thing, not the easy one."

"You agree?" Chris asked, surprised at how hard it was to get the words out. His diaphragm seemed to be trembling, and someone had interrupted the power to his legs.

"We're all in this together, Skip, you should know that." The chorus of affirmative noises sounded buzzing and distant in his ear. He hadn't realised quite how much he was fighting for until the prize had been won, thank God. If he'd known—if he'd truly known what was at stake, the responsibility would have paralysed him.

Dawn was hurrying. There was a golden haze in the east, like dust motes caught in sunshine, and the whole sky over there twinkled. Chris breathed in and out, and felt glad to be alive, and willing to die—a gorgeous, buoyed-up, light-as-air feeling, filling all the spaces his earlier terror had scoured clean.

Under the Hill: Dogfighters

He turned the plane for another pass, found Liadain's new mount at the throat of Flynn's beast. The girl on its back was half-supporting Oonagh, whispering something to her. She seemed less boneless now, but she was clearly not recovered enough to hold her own spear. Flynn was doing that for her, standing upright with his feet braced in the stirrups and fighting Liadain off with wide, dangerous swipes of the spear.

In single combat, he was getting the worst of it, she was so much faster than he was. Doubtless if a single blow of his had connected, she would have been knocked flat, tumbled off her dragon, and that would have been the end of it. But his blows couldn't connect, she was always in a different place. Always just dodging away, flicking in her trident in little taps that scarcely connected, but it would only take one of them to rip through the flying jacket and graze his skin with its venom, and the battle would be over.

It offended Chris to see Geoff fighting. For a man of war, he was the gentlest soul Chris had ever met. He gritted his teeth and pulled his now-usual trick of flying low, directly underneath the more tender scales of the green dragon's belly.

The front and upper gunners got off a rattling volley, and then everything went horribly wrong. Liadain's dragon let go of Oonagh's and simply fell, straight down on top of Chris's plane. The claws at the knee joint dug in to the wood and fabric wings of the Mosquito. Its long tail lashed around, curved, and the pointed tip of it thrust like a scorpion's sting through the rear-gun turret of the ghost Lanc. Perspex shattered in an eerie silence. When he heard the grunt, the coughing gurgle of Red with the stinger through his chest, Chris tried to get up, to run to him, and Hank's chill hands held him down.

"Dead already," he said soberly. "Nothing you can do but fly, Skipper."

171

Chris wasn't sure how the kite was staying in the air with the weight of the dragon pressing it down. The lift of the mighty Lancaster engines must have somehow been holding the Mosquito up too, but he could feel the wings bending upwards, the slow, soggy, cumbersome response of the stick. Up above, the mid-upper turret rattled into silence. "Run out, Skip. Made a ruddy great hole in it, but it's just taking it."

"Okay, Mid-upper. Get down to the rear and see what you can do for Red."

The dragon's fore-claws were closed about the join between wings and fuselage. It had been nosing at the propellers, trying to decide if it could bite there, lost a whisker and withdrawn. Now it braced its long, muscular neck, turned its head upside down and looked at him through the cockpit screen. Venom hit the Perspex like heavy rain. One good bite and the long fangs would sheer the front of the plane off, chomp him up. This was obviously no time for half measures.

Chris flipped the kite onto her back, dropped the altitude and scraped the dragon through Liadain's army, flinging armoured warriors and their weapons at the beast's head at one hundred miles an hour. Debris hit the props and was flung back, shattering the windscreen. The plane yowled and shuddered, the smell of overheating engines and dope and oily, metallic dragon's blood rang in his head like a single, high-pitched piercing note. And then many things happened at once.

The dragon let go, tried to twist in the air and failed. It slammed into the ground upside down and ploughed onwards thirty feet, raising a crater in the gorsy field. Free of the weight, the Mosquito kicked upwards five hundred feet in a single bound, making Chris's head feel like an overripe tomato ready to burst. He had not brought a flying suit, and the blood was pooling in his head, covering his vision with a film of red, making his pulse hammer, hammer, hammer at his skull with a pile driver.

He flipped the plane upright again, tried to master the dizziness, the protest of his neck and spine, the red, whining tremble of all his muscles. Saved him though it had, the ghost Lanc was not a light plane by any means, had to be wrestled through acrobatics by sheer brute force, and he was not as young as he used to be. He could feel exhaustion welling out of his bones like the onset of depression, grey and numb and hopeless, and he still hurt all over from the memory of that strange duel for Ben's soul that he wasn't completely sure he'd won.

Blue flames trickled from the outer port engine of the Lanc, and he wondered idly how that could be, what dimension the dead existed in, which could simultaneously be in this world and not. "Did we get her?"

"Bomb aimer here, Skip. I think we did. The dragon's crumpled up, looking pretty dead to me. I see her arm and shoulder. They're trying to get her out, but she's right underneath. Squashed flat."

"Well, that's..." He made for the road. With the port outer engine feathered and the starboard inner crushed, the power of the Lanc was no longer adequate to keep the mangled Mosquito in the air. Chris held on to her with sweating hands, fighting the juddering stick and the sloppy rudder, trying to figure out how to land two different planes at the same time. Heat blew in along with the wind and pieces of the windscreen peppered his face. He didn't think he could keep her in the air any longer. And where, but where, was the RAF?

They juddered to a halt on the tarmac, the engines sputtering out in what felt like a sudden solid wall of silence. Electrics fizzed by Chris's ears as he put his head in his hands and awarded himself the count of three to rest. Then he scrambled out, jumped down onto the road and stood in numb horror, realising that once again he had underestimated the problem.

The lights in the east, which he had taken for an unusual morning mist, were now zipping towards the battlefield like comets. It was another army, an army of the air, all clothed in brilliant silks and golden armour, with wings at their backs—metal feathered wings that beat like cymbals and tuned bells, so that his head was bemused by snatches of music. They had arrows and spears, henna-dyed beards, and fierce and beautiful faces. And it occurred to him that this—this flying glory of sound and strength and beauty—this must be Ben's heritage, the terrible fate he had rescued Ben from.

The ability to fly! God, if someone had rescued him from that, he'd never speak to them again. Somehow everything he could offer—a love so obviously torn, a messy house and a job that provided plenty of opportunities to die in nasty ways for a small payment and unlimited ridicule... Well, it didn't amount to much, if this was what was stacked on the other side. No wonder Ben was finding it difficult to choose.

The golden warriors descended on the battlefield like shooting stars. Five of them streaked towards the black dragon, where a now-recovered Oonagh reflected the dawn's blue light in a pillar of bronze and copper armour. The man at point raised his bow and shot the spear out of Oonagh's hand. She was still looking astonished when they grabbed her, blocked Flynn's punch almost contemptuously, picked up the girl beside him and flew away, to where their king waited, beneath a pavilion of scarlet silk that was still having its guy ropes hammered in.

Chris turned back to his plane. He didn't know if he could get it off the ground again, let alone what he could do if all the ammo was already gone. The slowly broadening light had washed away all traces of the phantom Lancaster. He could only see the Mosquito, looking badly beaten, with scorch marks around its tail, the rudder hanging half off, holes in the side and the cockpit, and long scores down both wings—claw marks two inches deep.

"Boys, are you there?"

Nothing. The wrecked interior was empty and the radio didn't even hiss in his ear any more. He had no idea what he could do to rescue the one known quantity in this mess from this new threat, but he picked up the crowbar he'd stashed behind his seat and went to try to find out.

Chapter Ten

As he grabbed fruitlessly for Oonagh, watched her be carried away between Chitrasen's soldiers, oddly pliant in their grasp, something shifted in Flynn's head. He was, for the first time, on his own with the dragon. He looked down and found it looking up at him, its tilted eye serious as it had never been before.

"Now is the time for this pretence to end," it said, half inside his skull, half whispered on lavender flame. At the words, the presence inside Flynn's head writhed and snapped its bonds as if they had been cobwebs. Flynn recoiled back into himself with a start and was finally, resoundingly, alone in his own head.

"You could have done that at any time," he realised.

"Of course. But now my queen needs me, and I have no desire to pander to your delusions any more. We go to her."

Suiting actions to words, Kanath hunched his powerful shoulders as he gave a dozen mighty flaps of his wings, driving them speeding past the combat below, taking them towards the pavilion, bare seconds behind Oonagh and her captors.

"Fine by me, old chap. Why did you let us get away with it in the first place?" But he thought he knew. Oonagh believed in the prophecy, that if he was fated to be on her side, on her side he would be whatever his beliefs. She had continued her policy of giving him enough rope to hang himself. And if she hadn't, would she have known enough about Liadain's movements to be here, giving her all in the defence of earth?

"Because the queen trusts those she has chosen to trust, and you were amongst that number. You did not prove unworthy to her at her hour of need—she would not be alive now if it were not for you. So you see her wisdom?"

"I have to admit I was mistaken about her. But you lying to me didn't make it any easier to find that out."

The dragon came roaring down upon the warriors in front of the pavilion, laying down a scorching path of blue fire. It set itself down on the blackened earth in front of Chitrasen's throne, interposing itself between the king and his guards. Stretching out a claw it managed to suggest, wordlessly, that Oonagh might easily elbow her captor in the throat and run from the ground to its wrist, elbow, shoulder and thence back into her saddle.

In fact she did none of those things. She only smiled up at Kanath and Flynn both, held out a hand made more regal by the fact that it was gloved in her enemies' blood, and said, "King Chitrasen, may I introduce my good friend, Kanath of the line of Oriel, and my champion, Flynn the Navigator."

"I lie to you?" the dragon asked with a rumble of laughter. "When did I do such a thing? Still, you do not feel vindicated, to have worked out the puzzle by yourself?"

"I mostly feel confused." Flynn almost forgot himself and jumped down onto the scrubby, weed-choked grass of earth. The smell of it alone was making his bottom lip tremble. The thought of never touching it again was like a ravenous hunger, sticking his belly to his backbone, not leaving space for air or thought. "Um, Queen Oonagh, are we not meant to be rescuing you at this point?"

The dragon's mere presence on the hill had altered the balance of power. The Gandharvas guarding Oonagh sensibly edged away from her, and she filled the extra space with charisma. Every line of her from the proudly held head to her copper-shod boots proclaimed that she was a queen, not a captive, that she was here by her own will and would depart by it if she so wished.

Given that Oonagh's bodyguard were only being kept from death at the hands of the angry mass of Liadain's grieving followers by a line of Chitrasen's troops, the queen's pose of untouchable power was, Flynn thought, a triumph of style over substance. Its doomed and futile quality gave it a certain magnificence, however.

Nor was he the only one to appreciate it. All this time, the king of the golden warriors had done no more than sit and watch, with his hands steepled in front of his face, his index fingers touching his lips. He had a harsh and thoughtful face, like that of a warrior and a scholar, and his armour was as silver as his beard, cool in that host of gold-clad warriors.

He had not yet moved to welcome his daughter, who stood just to the right of Oonagh, quite still in her ring of guards, with her bright open face smoothed into no expression at all, smudges on her cheeks and her long hair tangled down her back from the swim they had taken together through the sewers. She'd rolled the overlong legs of Flynn's overalls up to calf height, and her bare feet were dirty and poised as ever, even on the grass of earth.

From where he sat, perched on top of the dragon, Flynn watched as Ben left the knot of Oonagh's fighters who had been protecting him, walked slowly and perhaps reluctantly through the army, up the hill towards the throne. Flynn could see the wave of recognition, the shock and then the decision to give homage, that went through each Gandharva warrior as he got in Ben's way. He could see too the way Ben flinched every single time, as though he had been hoping to be stopped, rejected and given the perfect excuse to run away.

Just on the edge of the field, Geoff could also see the dirty blond hair of the skipper. The real-life, flesh-and-blood, non-imaginary skipper, gleaming bright as a sovereign for a moment as he climbed into an early sunbeam, swinging over the field's boundary, jumping down again, stiffly, moving as if weariness had settled into his bones.

And maybe Flynn had made up the whole parachute-harness thing? He hadn't been thinking terribly clearly when it happened—he'd been chased, and he hadn't had the time to look properly. It had been dark when he threw the thing through the portal. He might have seen it wrong, remembered it wrong. He might be sitting here afraid to touch the green earth for no good reason at all. Wild and painful hope swelled in him. He knew it was false and cherished it anyway.

"My daughter," said Chitrasen at last, his voice rounded and full as that of a trained singer. "Approach."

Sumala's hands twitched as though she had gone to raise them to smooth down her hair, realised the futility of the gesture. She paced slowly beneath the awning of the pavilion, until she was close enough to bend down and touch her father's feet. She still looked doubtful, guarded, and Flynn's tender feelings ached for her. He knew too well that there was never any going back.

Then, as if to prove him wrong, the king broke out into a huge smile, rose and flung his arms around her. She stiffened, resentful for a moment, before putting her head in the hollow of his shoulder, letting him touch the single jewel that hung in the middle of her forehead, the only thing she had left of her untold riches. "Did she clothe you like this? This woman, did she do this to you?"

"No, Father. I swam out of the city to freedom. I could not float while wearing so much gold."

"Do you know how much I worried about you?"

"I'm sorry, Father. I didn't mean to cause you anxiety."

"Of course you didn't. It was this woman and her people. I knew when they first came to me, begging for my help, that she was up to no good. But now you are safe again, you can watch as she is punished and be satisfied that justice has been done."

Sumala turned, looked at Oonagh and then up at Flynn. "Y-es," she said, drawing the word out into a space in which she could think. "Flynn, why are you sitting up there still? Come down. I want to introduce you to my father." She gave the king a sideways glance and a smile that brought out dimples in her cheeks.

"Flynn has been my champion, Father. He's helped me ever since we met. I think he should be rewarded." She turned the smile on Flynn, but when he didn't move, it faltered. Frowning now, she balanced on one foot and rubbed the other on her calf. It caught in the rolled-up trouser-leg, making the fabric untuck. "Come on. Why don't you come down? You don't need to be afraid any more."

She stamped her foot prettily, though the effect was not the same without her many bells. Flynn almost obeyed, swaying forward without thinking, obedient to the tone of threatened hurt. But her stamp had completed the unravelling of her trouser-leg. The fabric slowly slid down her leg and pooled around her foot, touching the ground.

Flynn wished he'd been wrong, but here in the broadening daylight, with no darkness to blame and no present threat, he could see it quite clearly. The moment the fabric of his overalls touched the ground the material instantly discoloured, turning from blue to a dingy, decayed brown. When she moved, even slightly, the trouser-leg tore like wet paper, separating from the better material above it.

Yet the stain was spreading slowly upwards. When the knee tore out, Sumala finally looked down, followed his gaze. She breathed in, a hiss through clenched teeth, and bent to touch the decayed material. It separated beneath her fingers, leaving her with handfuls of brown flyaway thread that turned further into dust with every moment.

When she looked up again, there was such pity in her gaze that Flynn had to close his eyes and turn his face away to hide the anguish.

"I lost nearly seventy years living in Faerie," he said, feeling the words lock the knowledge down, make it real. A trap he'd sprung on himself, a fucking fairytale irony that he should have *known* was going to happen to him. And God, it wasn't as though he hadn't been warned. He'd read Rip Van Winkle in his youth. It just wasn't quite as funny from the inside. "And I traded another hundred for the powder to open the portal. The material's a hundred and seventy years old in this world, and I'm almost two hundred. If I ever set foot in my home again"—he nodded at the handful of decomposed fabric she was still holding out to him, as though he could somehow turn it back with a wish—"that's what will happen to me."

"Oh, Flynn!" She smeared dust over her face as she wiped her eyes. "So that's why you wouldn't come when we had the chance to leave, earlier?"

"You should have gone without me."

"I didn't know." She shook her head. "But then why..." As she was struggling for words, one of the older, bearded warriors standing behind the king's throne took off his outer garment—a long coat of pink silk, stitched with pearls—and passed it to her. Looking at the way age was creeping inexorably over the coveralls, wicking up from the ground like water to soak the whole garment, she shrugged into the coat and pinned it closed with a brooch of moonstone. "Why did you come out here with me? Why didn't you stop trying to find a way out?"

"Because you could still get home, and I wanted to help you," Flynn answered. But it was a partial truth at best, and he'd had enough of holding back doubts and uncomfortable truths. What did any of it matter now? He might as well be perfectly honest—there was nothing left to lose.

"And because I was trying to tell myself I was wrong. That perhaps when I got back it wouldn't be that bad. Perhaps I'd been mistaken. Perhaps there would be a way. Except that now I'm too bloody scared to put a foot down. I want to talk to my skipper first. There are things..."

Evidently he had not yet reached the depths of the pit quite yet. The new abyss that opened at this thought made him feel like he were sinking in the North Sea in the wreckage of the plane. He could feel the water coming in, and the pressure, and the cold. "There are things I've got to tell him."

"Like what?" asked a voice. The ranks of bodyguards who formed a living wall around the pavilion parted, and Ben walked through. He was clean shaven, with the neat modern haircut and the tan line of a watch strap around his wrist, but Flynn's first reaction was to think, bitterly, *He has no problem coming home* because Ben fitted in here like a jewel into its setting. The slight coarseness of his humanity, the flesh and blood warmth and its imperfections only showed on a second glance. But when they did Flynn was ashamed of himself—ashamed of his jealousy, of his envy, and the selfishness they must have grown out of.

You should be bloody hoping he's on the level. But "should be" was as far as he could take it, today. He could acknowledge that his own stupid decisions weren't Ben's fault. But he couldn't shift the iron ball of envy and grief and loss out of his throat by any more than that.

Ben wanted to have that conversation, but there were other things that needed dealing with first, and he should have addressed them. He turned back to face the throne, resumed his measured walk towards it, trying to hide the fact that he was so nervous it had passed beyond a feeling and become an altered state of consciousness. He felt slightly flayed, a layer of skin missing and everything that much more intense.

The experience of being surrounded by people like him, of belonging, was almost suffocating. Only now did he realise how used he'd been to being the outsider, the lone wolf, and he felt as though some part of his personality was being crushed by familiarity. The cool, unwelcoming look of the man on the throne was almost a balm in this situation, soothing him. Perhaps it was that which convinced him that whatever he'd been in another life, he was his own man now.

Ben came to a halt next to Oonagh and dipped his head in a tiny nod of acknowledgement.

"Karshni," said the man the elf king. Gandharva. Whatever.

"Bless you," Ben replied facetiously, and could have laughed at the discovery that his protective prickliness did not go away under pressure. He hoped for anger or amusement in return—those he would have known how to deal with, would have felt that at least some personal connection had been made.

183

The king, however, only looked puzzled, and said carefully, "It is your name, my son."

"My name is Ben." It felt good to have it out in the open in front of all these witnesses. "I have no idea what I was before, but in this life I am not..."

Oonagh moved, darting forward and jostling him as she came. She stood closer than he found comfortable, both hands wrapped about his elbow. It occurred to him that the battle had only been a precursor to this—a way of getting this meeting to happen—that perhaps he shouldn't pre-emptively ruin it. But it was hard not to flinch.

"Good," Oonagh interrupted. "Now you are present, Karshni, we can come to some peaceable resolution. Put aside your anger and let us give thought to how we can solve the problems of all our worlds."

Chitrasen leaned forwards and stroked the rubies knotted into his beard. His dark eyes flashed with something that was half-anger, half-intrigue. "Why do you presume to speak for me? You are my prisoner, shortly to be tried and executed for holding my daughter hostage, for turning my son against me. What makes you think you have the right to advise me, like a free woman?"

Oonagh smiled at him, took one hand away and pushed the mass of diamond hair back from her face, "When Karshni left you," she said, settling the hand on her abdomen protectively, "you told him that he must find a royal bride and give you grandchildren. That is exactly what he has done—trying to demonstrate, through his obedience, his love for you and his wish to be taken back into your favour. It is true we are not wed, yet, but you will surely not wish to execute the mother of your grandson?"

Everything Ben had been sure about, everything he'd wanted to say—*get lost, you and I have nothing in common, I am not your plaything and I want nothing to do with you*—crumpled in his chest, leaving a vacuum that waited to be filled by something huge. He wondered what it was going to be.

"What?" he said, at the same instant that Chitrasen's look of blank shock became a forced laugh.

"The boy is a degenerate. If he had been willing to fulfil his duty to me by marrying and having children I would not have..." he waved a disapproving hand at Ben, taking in his top-to-toe humanity, "...done *this* to him."

Ben looked away, gathering his wits and his temper. From atop the hill where they stood, he could see past the ring of Chitrasen's bodyguards and out into the clear light of a fine day in the Peaks. Where the field met the roads another rank of Chitrasen's army had been drawn up, and between the two ranks of Gandharva warriors, Liadain's people had formed themselves into lines, one facing in, one out. There seemed for the moment to be a standoff. Liadain's surviving commanders were in a huddle in the centre of the Nine Ladies, presumably discussing who was to lead them now she was gone.

A distant sound of traffic rumbled from the A5, and on the side of the hill closest to the stile, Chris was speaking urgently to a group of Gandharva guards. As Ben watched, they searched him for weapons, relieved him of a crowbar and began to lead him up towards the pavilion.

Ben wanted all this business sorted before Chris arrived. He stood on tiptoe and whispered angrily into Oonagh's ear, "I don't know what you're trying to achieve, but he is going to go ballistic when he finds out it isn't true."

"I am trying to achieve what I have always been trying to achieve," she said, smiling down at him. Her hair swung

185

forwards and touched his face, and each little strand felt like an electric shock. "Peace between your people—*both* your peoples—and mine. Energy for my ships, and thus a way out for my subjects from the madness and desolation in which they find themselves."

His gaze flicked to Chris again, and she watched it with a smile. "And what makes you think it isn't true?"

"I never touched you!" Ben didn't like this game. There was a kind of horror in it he wasn't willing to put a name to, but it chimed with all the paranoia and body horror of *The X-files* in his head. He ran through his recent memories looking for drugged invasion, anaesthesia, something scrubbed and medical and sharp.

Oonagh turned him by the elbow so that they were facing away from the king. She bent her head, shadowed by the pavilion, and when she did so the shadows ran over her face like falling rain. Ben found himself, just for an instant, looking back at indigo eyes rather than amethyst, a wider, heavier brow and jaw, skin of snow rather than obsidian. His stomach lurched and he bit his lip, fighting the reaction down, feeling shock tremble through all his cells. "Arran? You...?"

The second face was swept effortlessly away, but he couldn't look at her now without seeing the resemblance, the very faint resemblance of expression and composition—the line of the mouth, and the little scar he had touched on Arran's face that she hid beneath one of the triskeles on her cheek. She had, even, something of Arran's kindness beneath the satisfaction in her eyes. And every bit of the same joy in her own cleverness.

"Did I not tell you that I went about among my people in disguise? And you imagined what? That I would merely change clothes? It did not occur to you to wonder why, in order to speak to you myself, I had to tell you I had sent him away? Nor why, being a noble in my service, he was not here in my army now?"

The nausea forced itself into Ben's throat again as he remembered that strange drugged night he had spent with Arran. It had been uncomfortable enough when he thought it had meant nothing. Now...now he knew she had done it deliberately as part of a plan, political leverage...his child...

"I don't..." he said. "I can't—"

"Well, this is good news!" Chitrasen had evidently been thinking hard too. There was doubt behind his eyes, but he rose to his feet with an expansive smile. "So my son has responded to correction and repented of his selfish ways? He has brought me a queen as a bride, and a grandson already on the way. Karshni, come here and receive your father's forgiveness."

Oh, and now Ben really wanted to throw up. He didn't know whether any of this man's joy was genuine, but he could take a shrewd guess that half of this "forgiveness" was massive politics. *Behold how wise your king is, who has lovingly chastised his son in order to save him from sin, and now shows his warm heart by taking the penitent child back.* You'd pay a million dollars for a publicity stunt like that in our world.

Yet, and yet, something in him, Karshni's fading voice perhaps, fiercely wanted to believe he had only been sent away for a little while. Not disowned at all, just briefly punished and now embraced. Maybe Ben was being unfair, and Chitrasen felt it too—desperately wanted his son back and was seizing a chance to do it without losing face.

Ben put his face in his hands. Oonagh's clever plans, and the armies standing silently around him, sizing one another up, they were closing in on him like an iron maiden, the spikes tightening and driving inwards. Trapped.

He could say *I don't want your forgiveness, old man. I am content as a human, and I'm still a fucking deviant. If you don't like it you can suck on it.* He could say that, and then the brief entente cordial between Oonagh and Chitrasen would be over. Chitrasen would wipe out the pathetic remnants of Oonagh's forces without breaking a sweat, take his daughter and go home, leaving Liadain's people at large. An army of vampires, turned on the North and spreading. If he wanted to retain his pride, that was the price.

And there was a child. The thought put out delicate leaves, pushed them through the hard crust of his heart and unfurled a very tiny bud of wonder. *His* child. How proud that would have made his real mother. She had wished only for his happiness when she found out what he was, but she had still not been able to resist stopping every pram she passed so she could coo at the infant within. She had not been able to conceal, sometimes, how much she'd wished for a grandchild of her own. Ben did not believe heaven did not admit those without descendants, but he did hope that wherever she was now, this news had made her happy.

Chitrasen still stood in the centre of the pavilion, surrounded by advisers and generals, with his hands outstretched and the smile beginning to slip from his lips. *I'll do it for* my *Dad,* Ben thought fiercely, *my untouchable, awesome Dad, because I didn't get the chance to say goodbye.*

He walked slowly forwards, hesitated and was engulfed in a bear hug that almost cracked his ribs. A moment's stiffness, and a very faint memory washed over him of those same hands covering his own, the fingers guiding his fingers over his first flute, in a place full of tawny light and music. Just for an instant he let himself relax, brought his hands up and hugged back, looking up into a face that reminded him startlingly of his own.

"I don't really remember you," he said, and wondered too late if it had been cruel.

Chitrasen smiled, though the edge of careful calculation never dulled behind his eyes. Perhaps it was a kingly thing—constant mindfulness. Oonagh had the same look at times. "That will sort itself out in time. And time is something of which we have unlimited resources. Now, I understand you are having problems with a rebellion?"

Ben looked out at Liadain's nobles. Their purposeful huddle had broken apart, leaving a willow-green girl alone in the centre of the stones. She raised a hand around which there twisted a circle of white light, lowered it and pushed it onto her throat, where it rested, becoming a torc of silver. A great roar of approval went up from Liadain's army, and as the green girl gave a shrill battle cry, they turned and threw themselves at the ranks of Gandharva soldiers with recharged fury.

"As you can see." Ben said. "Is there some way of stopping them getting loose on this world? They don't belong here."

"Easily done." The king put out a hand, and from the knot of his advisers a warrior in cloth of gold came carrying a great curved bow. A Brahmin in an austere white linen *dhoti* followed him, bearing an ornately carved wooden box. When he opened it, there was a single arrow inside. Chitrasen took it and set it to his bow, drew back and aimed unhurriedly for the centre of the battle.

He loosed the arrow, and Ben watched it fly burning magnesium bright against a sky that held—about a mile away—a single stationary helicopter. The arrow landed harmlessly on the ground. Chitrasen smiled, dusted off his hands and gave the bow back to his attendant.

"What?" Ben began, choking it off as Oonagh returned to his side, squeezed the arm she had already bruised.

"Look."

It was still just a scrum to Ben's eyes, but then he noticed something strange. Liadain's men were slowly faltering, drawing apart. They looked at one another, aghast, and then with a roar of confusion and betrayal they began to fight each other.

The effect of the arrow slowly worked its way through Liadain's army, setting them against each other. There was little to do but simply watch as the force imploded. Eventually there was nothing but the vampires left. Watching *them* destroy each other was too gory for Ben's stomach.

Turning away from the sight, Ben caught sight of Chris again. He had worked his way through slow negotiation to the top of the hill. At Ben's waved hand, the final two ranks of bodyguards parted to allow him through.

Chris reached the dais, propped himself, insouciantly—Ben thought rather magnificently—on Kanath's shoulder. He glanced from Ben up to Flynn on the dragon's back, and his open face was a picture of weariness and bafflement and hurt when neither of them moved towards him. Ben smiled at least, but Flynn bit his lower lip and looked away.

Behind Chris, the field was rapidly clearing of enemies, even the corpses whisping away into vapour or crumbling into the soil. The drone of the helicopter had grown closer. Ben could see it now, a large, military-looking thing with two rotors, rockets mounted on its sides and the muzzles of rocket launchers in its snub nose. Trust the cavalry to come too late, he thought, as it began to lower itself down next to Chris's beaten-up Mosquito.

Chitrasen was watching it too. "I must not be here," he said. "This is no longer an age of wonders, and the intercourse of our two worlds is strictly discouraged by the gods."

He nodded quietly to his attendants, allowing them to rush off, shouting to their own subordinates. The Gandharva troops began to lift from the ground like autumn leaves, as copper red and gold as leaf fall. The wind took them and blew, and the lines of warriors skirled away exactly as leaves in a storm wind. Flickers of bright metal in the sky, and the clouds parted and swirled. Then they were gone, leaving Chitrasen and five of his followers alone with Oonagh, her warlord Bram, Kanath, Sumala and the three human men.

"Today my son is restored to me, thanks to you," Chitrasen said, taking Oonagh's hand. She allowed it graciously, but neither of their smiles reached their eyes. "And since we speak now in private, tell me of Arran. Is the boy still...involved with that man?"

"I don't believe he will willingly ever associate with Arran again," said Oonagh with a touch of sadness. "Those days ended with his banishment."

She tilted her head to the side and looked at Ben sidelong, her gaze sliding to Chris. "He has changed since he became human. As have I. You will find me a faithful friend, and my people will remember that we are indebted to you."

With a great clank, the helicopter lowered its side to let a man in RAF blue walk out onto the torn-up grass.

"Perhaps we should continue this discussion elsewhere," said Chitrasen. "When you have dealt with your enemies at home and set your house in order, come and visit me. Bring my grandson. We will talk about this plan of yours to find new worlds. There are many ambitious youngsters in my own realm who would be glad of estates of their own. Until then."

He clapped his hands together and was gone as though he'd snuffed himself out like a candle flame. It was so sudden even Kanath started, spitting a little yellow acid out of his flared nostrils and twitching the end of his forked tail.

"I too should not be here," said Oonagh. "Bram, take what remains of the army back through. I will come last and close the portal behind us."

It was a bedraggled party of injured elves and one half-crippled dragon that limped back through the gap beneath the hill, squirming into the darkness under the soil.

"Will you return with me?" said Oonagh to Ben at last, wiping a smear of blood from between her fingers.

"I don't *have to*?"

She gazed at Chris again, with that look of half-amusement, half-wariness. "No. Your freedom has been bought and paid for. Never let it be said that I know 'how this works' less than some flitting mortal. Come if you want. Stay if you want. But if you stay, your son will never know his father."

"You…are the coldest bitch I have ever—"

"I am a queen. I have no wants, no desires, but for the welfare of my people. If you were not so much a younger son, you would understand this."

There was an echo from another life, and Ben had had too much pride in that life, retained too much pride in this, to allow anyone to talk to him like that. "No," he said, "I'm not coming with you. Haven't you understood that everything I've done since you wandered back into my life was to get rid of you? All right, I'll play nice in front of my father for the sake of the world, but don't think there's anything more in it than that. So yes, I *do* understand, and if you need me to play escort when you visit the old man, then I'll come. I know what responsibility is too. But don't get the idea there's anything personal in it, because I want you the fuck out of my life."

Oonagh laughed. "We are not as dissimilar as you would like to think."

Then she patted Kanath's nose and looked up into Flynn's grey and world-weary face. "But you will come with me, Navigator. You justified the trust I had in you and saved my life. I will lavish you with honours, when we get home."

"Flynn's not going back there." Alone out of the host, Sumala had stayed, though she wore a pair of golden wings now and carried another pair in one hand. "He's coming with me."

"He bloody well is not!" Chris reached up the dragon's side, tried to close his hand around Flynn's ankle, and drew it back empty when Flynn moved hastily out of the way.

Chris looked at the palm of his hand for what seemed a long time, then put it down and rubbed it carefully against his trouser leg. When he looked up again there was something painfully fragile about his face, open almost to the bone. "Flynn...and Ben...are staying. The hell. With me. That's the whole point. That's the whole fucking point. You're staying the hell with me."

For Flynn, the urge to reach down and wrap his hand around Chris's was like the urge to breathe—it only got stronger the more it was denied. Flynn had thought the hag's nails had been the worst pain he'd ever experienced in his life, but this was worse. This was the end of the world for him, and he could feel it tearing apart. All the fabric of his life was unravelling, leaving him to hold the frayed edges together with half of him missing, destroyed.

But he wasn't going to go and leave the skipper in doubt—leave him to come back and try another rescue. The man had his life to live. He had a future. Hell, he'd even lived over a decade without Geoff already, so this wouldn't come as too much of a shock for him. Probably even be a relief.

Looking down at Chris's terrified face gave the lie to that thought, made it bloody obvious it would be nothing of the sort. So he didn't look. He took a deep breath and coughed to clear the obstruction from his throat. "I'm not coming back."

"What?"

It had been a weak and thin little whisper, he supposed, but even so the man shouldn't make him say it again. The flare of miserable anger helped him to raise his head, look the skipper in the eye and repeat it. "I'm not coming back, Skip."

Oh, and there was the flinch he'd been afraid of, hazel eyes gone dark with anguish. Chris looked away, concealing the expression, rubbed a hand over his face. "Why?"

He could have told the truth. He intended to, at first. But that would have led to further rescue attempts, maybe even to Chris offering to do the unthinkable and come with him.

Oh God, please yes!

And he was not going to be selfish about this. He gave himself a mental kick, thinking of that scene he'd been shown in the restaurant—Chris and Ben laughing together, looking at ease and happy. He was already a third wheel in Chris's life, no sense in making things worse for all of them.

"I found someone else." He gestured towards Sumala, hoped she would hold her tongue and not deny it. This was not the time for another one of her regular I-can't-be-involved-with-a-disgusting-human outbursts. Perhaps there was a little of her soul still left in him at that, because although she raised her head and gave him a piercing gaze, she said nothing.

"But..." Chris had raised both hands to cover his mouth. The words came out muffled and unsure. "You called me. You wanted to come home—"

"Skipper..."

"It was going to be like the old days." Chris gave him an imploring look, far too young and vulnerable for that mature face. "You called me to help you come home."

God, he felt like a fucking heel. The effort to keep his lips from trembling, to keep his eyes dry, meant his face felt like a board, stiff and stern and fierce, and he didn't want this to be his final farewell—to take out Chris's heart and stamp it into the ground—but it was for his own good. Wasn't it?

"I called you because of the invasion," he said, carefully coaxing his voice out, willing it to show nothing of what he felt. The result was harsh, angry. "Not because of us. Skipper, we both knew that was a temporary thing while the war was on." He beckoned, and Sumala passed him up the winged harness. He examined the buckles rather than look down.

"It was a bit of fun because things were...tense." He'd started filling the silence because he couldn't bear to listen to it, and the worst thing was he still wanted to lean down and touch the skipper one last time. Just to say goodbye. Touch the ends of his hair. Even a handshake. And he daren't. Because Chris was like the soil, he was part of this world now. If he touched the man, if he allowed himself to be touched, he'd gain one hundred and seventy years in an instant, crumble in the man's hand, and he was not willing to do that either to Chris or to himself.

But his hands cramped from holding them back and his ribs ached from how much they yearned to be hugged tight and never let go again, and he shoved the wings on haphazard, unable to take this a moment longer.

"It never really meant anything. You know that."

He didn't think he could feel any smaller, any more abject, until he looked down and found there were tears in Chris's eyes. Their gazes locked, and something passed on them—an understanding of sorts. He latched the final buckle. Chris sniffed, rubbed his tattered cuff along his eyes and straightened up. "I suppose I did. I'm sorry to make a scene. Good luck then, Geoff. I wish you all the best."

He wanted to say something that would make it better. Couldn't think of a thing. "You too, Skipper." He racked his brains for that perfect phrase, was still trying to find it when Sumala alighted on the dragon's back and showed him how to fly. He could have hated her at that moment, if it wasn't all being stored up for use against himself, because of course there wasn't anything he could say or do that would make this better. The only thing that might make it a tiny bit easier on them both was to get it done and over so that it didn't keep hurting like a bitch, so they could move on and get a start on the recovery.

There was no joy in flight, but there would have been no joy in anything for him. He set the wings working, rose up with a friendly wave, teeth still embedded in the side of his cheek to keep him from blubbing. Chris gave him an equally friendly salute and a painfully artificial smile, and he turned away quick and found the nearest cloud to cover him, so that when Sumala joined him she would not know how much of the wet on his face was tears.

"I won't marry you, you know," she said, touching his arm with sympathy, "but father will find a nice girl of your own rank for you. Come on, they are all waiting for us." But when he hugged her tight and bent his head into her shoulder to weep, she didn't hurry him up, and she didn't make him let go.

Drained of tears and options, he followed her to where her people waited, and thence into her world. He didn't look back—it would have been more than he could take.

Ben had never seen anyone completely fall apart before. Chris did it very neatly. Indeed, if Oonagh hadn't chosen that moment to turn to him and say farewell, Ben might not have noticed it happening at all. Chris stood quite upright, as if he were on parade, but there was nothing behind his eyes, he didn't seem to even hear Oonagh's words to him.

She broke off, midway through a courteous speech of thanks to give Ben a thoughtful look. "You choose to stay with this man?"

"Yes." It wasn't a hard decision, with Chris looking so very stricken, so very much like he was holding it together only because he didn't know any other way to handle this much grief.

"I think that's wise. For you don't like to lie, and if you came with me you would have to, constantly."

"I don't like to lie, and I don't like to be lied to. I don't like to be fucking trapped, no matter how good your intentions." He offered her a hand up, to get on the dragon's back, but it was more out of a desire to be rid of her than from courtesy. She didn't look very pregnant, but then he supposed she wouldn't, this soon. "Besides, you've taken enough that was his. I'm going to make sure he has at least something left."

Oonagh laughed, exchanged one long glance with the man from the helicopter, who was currently slogging his way uphill, picking through the tossed boulders on his way towards them. "You have a softer heart than you allow to show." She nudged the dragon with her knees and tossed him the circlet he had worn. He didn't attempt to catch it and it lay at his feet gleaming like water. "We'll meet again, Karshni, even if it is after both of you are dead. I can afford to wait."

Chris lost what seemed an infinite gap of time, came back to himself at the sound of a man's voice, calling "Mr. Gatrell?" in a clipped, authoritarian tone. Oonagh must have said something—some form of farewell, for he could see her bending low to the dragon's back as the two of them squirmed into the side of the hill. The dragon's tail grated against small pebbles as it dragged inside and a fall of dry soil and small flint tumbled after it. Then there was nothing on the hilltop but himself and Ben and the man from the helicopter, striding up through the stones with an expression on his face that said he was prepared to take responsibility for this success if it was absolutely thrust upon him.

Chris thought he should be angry about that. The stripes at the man's shoulders told him he should be at least standing to attention, but he really couldn't see the point of either. It was Ben who said, "If you're the cavalry, you're a little late," in a voice whose tartness brought a certain dim satisfaction to Chris's soul. Not the only one feeling shell-shocked and resentful, then. That was good.

"You called for backup but it seems you didn't need it."

Chris put two and two together. "Air Vice-Marshal." He roused himself to nod, but the salute still adamantly refused to come. "Maybe if you'd come sooner there'd be another pilot still alive. How long have you been here, observing?"

The brass had a leathery face, and the sort of thick silver hair Chris associated with aging movie stars. "Long enough," he said. "I presume this is Mr. Chaudhry?"

Was it, though? Chris wondered. Ben was not demonstrative at the best of times, and the little hurt of that was subsumed in the larger devastation of Geoff's decision. But was it Ben or Karshni who stood with him, scowling?

"That's me." Ben didn't shake the outstretched hand. "What's it to you?"

"Only that the police have been treating your disappearance as murder." Henderson's bland face froze a little further. "I shall inform them they can call off the inquiry. But, gentlemen, if you weren't civilians I would have you on the carpet for your insolence."

"What are you going to do with us?" Chris thought about the last time the top brass had been involved: the psychiatric ward; trying to prove he was sane enough not to spend the rest of his life in an institution. He didn't think he had the energy to fight that particular battle again.

Perhaps Henderson recognised the weariness and grief after all, for he gave a small smile and looked around, taking in the wreckage of the Tornado, the Nine Ladies—only six left upright. The patches of blood on the grass were even now turning into rusty-red clover and field poppies.

"I'm going to send you home. Believe it or not, we have most of that on tape. In a few days you'll be asked to come in and give statements. Then you'll be sworn to secrecy and allowed to go about your business. I may, however, keep a closer eye on you in future."

He offered his hand to Chris, who took it automatically and was held in a firm, dry grip for a moment while the air vice-marshal fixed him with a bright blue gaze. "You're owed my thanks, though I don't suppose you want them. I can at least deal with the fallout for you."

He smiled. "For example, I believe you arrived in a stolen plane, and you, Mr. Chaudhry, arrived on a dragon. Let me give you a lift home. We'll talk in a couple of days."

Chapter Eleven

They dropped Ben in the scrubland a hundred metres from his own house, and under the curious stares of a dozen children and a dozen armed marines, he didn't want to push it by insisting on going home with Chris. The man himself said nothing either way, just looked at him with preoccupied eyes as if he was seeing something entirely different, out through the metal walls and seventy years ago.

"I'll…see you later," Ben managed before wading through the onlookers and heading home. But the big, neat house didn't feel like home to him any more. He shucked off his flamboyant silks in the hallway, hesitated over what to do with them and then shoved them in the washing machine as he passed it. The phone rang just as he was going upstairs, and he ignored it. It echoed up the stairs all the time he was throwing on jeans and a T-shirt, folding a suit into an overnight bag.

There was a whiskey glass in the sink that he didn't remember putting there, police tape over the tarpaulin that closed the gap where the extension had been. A new plywood door and padlock and the marks of big dirty boots on the carpet in what was left of the new living room. The wind came in from beneath the new door and eddied the scent of floral air freshener, and when he touched the door into the kitchen, greasy grey fingerprint powder came off on his hands.

I came back for this? He thought of the glory of the Gandharva army, of the beauty and discipline of Chitrasen's people, invincible and unashamed. It made him wonder what had been so terrible about his parents' upbringing that had made them want to reinvent themselves, leave their entire pasts behind. Made him wonder too what he was missing, whether it was too late to reconnect with his own heritage. He was a prince—bloody hell! A prince in exile. He could surely manage to do better than this empty imitation of someone else's life.

Ben moved the vase of now wilted flowers away from his parents' wedding photo, leaving it nakedly on display for the first time since it was taken. *Time for you to stop being ashamed,* he thought, looking at their youthful faces with love. Perhaps somewhere in the stack of letters and documents he had inherited with the house, he could find the names of his family left in India. It wasn't too late to get in touch. Instead of regretting his lack of community, he could get off his arse and find one.

And in the meantime he could also ask Chris whether his morris musicians could use a mandola player. It wasn't exactly a high-powered career in the record industry, but it was a small step towards getting music back into his life, and better than practicing alone.

The phone went again as he was passing back through the hall, and he noticed with some disbelief that it was only half past twelve. The afternoon stretched ahead as it always did. He felt that too should have changed—the way the world worked should not be trundling on, oblivious, when he felt transformed. Ignoring the phone, he locked the door behind him, flung the bag into his car and—with a sudden optimism towards his future—drove to Chris's house in Matlock.

It was shuttered tight, derelict looking, blinds down in the kitchen and bin-bags taped over the broken sitting room window. When he knocked on the door, he got a wall of silence for his trouble. He hammered harder. "Chris, are you in there?"

Time for a moment of panic—bloody hell, he knew he shouldn't have allowed the man to be alone, shouldn't have left him undefended, walking wounded as he was. Then Chris opened the door and stumbled over the threshold, already three quarters of the way towards falling-down drunk, his hair dishevelled and his eyes red rimmed in a pallid, haunted face.

"Thought you...thought you'd gone home. What'choo doing here? All over now, isn't it? So you can bugger off and...and so can I." It was half-belligerent and half-self-pitying, a very unattractive combination, but when Ben got his arm under Chris's shoulder, steered him back inside, the older man's body was loose and pliant against him. Trusting.

"Did you hit the bottle the moment you were in the door?" he asked, rhetorically.

"Hate drinking alone." Chris let himself be led into the sitting room, sat down on a cushion on the least vicious end of the sofa, where there was indeed a mostly-empty bottle of Irish whiskey and an ashtray filled with the ash and butts of five cigarettes. "Going to have to get used to it."

Ben registered the broken TV and the word *Murderer* sprayed on the wall in bright red paint. Shit. If he'd known Chris was coming back to *this*, there was no way he'd have let him go. To lose so much, fight so hard and then be kicked in the teeth with this when you got home... No wonder he'd turned to the booze with such abandon.

Chris hadn't washed, was sitting now bowed over with his elbows on his knees, his head in his hands, still in the burnt and battered black hoodie he'd worn for the rescue. It was torn in several places, framing bruises and dried blood. The hands, knotted in his hair, struck Ben suddenly as beautiful—cleverly articulated, perfectly made, slender and expressive—and stained reddish-brown.

Ben picked at the edges of the wallpaper. As he'd suspected, it had been there a long time. The glue was old and tired. He got his fingers in behind the paper and tore the whole panel off, ripping the red word into pieces, crumpling the pieces up and tossing them into the fireplace. He'd get a glazier in tomorrow for the window, paint this room. Something lighter than the current dingy stripes. Maybe he'd even get the chance to add those bookshelves, and the decent curtains he'd been itching to install since he first saw the place.

Chris flinched at the sound of tearing, and certainty and affection flooded up in Ben as though a dam had broken in his soul.

"Look at you." He shook his head. "You're a mess. A complete hero, and a fucking disaster area." Pulling Chris up by the arms, he pointed him in the direction of the stairs. "I'm going to put some coffee on, and then we're going to take a shower. I want you to drink lots of water and—"

"Not an invalid. Know how to hold my drink. Drink you under the table any time... What did you say?"

"I said you're a disaster—"

"Something about a shower?"

Ben surprised himself by laughing. God, he did, he felt happy. How had that happened? "I thought you'd like that idea. Feel free to throw up any time as long as it's not over me."

Chris's miserable face melted into a smile—a little tentative, a little bemused with itself, but radiant nonetheless. "You say the most romantic things."

The shower turned out to be awkward and strangely tender, Chris almost asleep in the warm spray, needing to be held up. Ben didn't know whether to feel insulted or charmed, decided that a combination of both summed up the entire relationship so far. And he must like it, mustn't he, or he wouldn't have come back for more.

Cleaned and wrapped in pyjamas and a big flannelette dressing gown Ben had found tucked away in the airing cupboard, Chris was a little more human. He curled into the corner of the sofa and cradled a cup of coffee, head bent over the steam, hair tousled and drying slowly in the close, midsummer heat. Ben felt a little more human himself once he had opened the kitchen blinds and windows to let in fresh sunlight and moving air. Then he phoned Phyllis and Grace to tell them they were back, not to worry, and please don't come around until tomorrow afternoon at the earliest.

When he'd made some lunch, which they ate in companionable silence, washed the plates and taken out the rubbish, he put his bag on the packing-crate coffee table and brought out the circlet from the depths of it. The silver jewel in the centre shone like a fallen star, washing his aching eyes and Chris's tired face in misty, cooling light.

"She'll be keeping tabs on you with that." Chris had raised his head only enough for the light to reflect from his half-open eyes. "You really want to keep it?"

"No. I just didn't want to leave it there for the police to find. D'you think I should give it to the RAF? For their X-files department, if they have one?"

"I think you should bury it. Out in the garden, under a marker." The smile was tired and a little worn around the edges. "She's clever. And...fond of you. Maybe there's more to it than meets the eye. You might find you need it later."

Ben went into the kitchen and returned with a glass of water and painkillers. He took one of the shelves from the crates and laid it over the springs of the sofa so that he could sit down next to Chris, wrap his fingers around the glass and make sure he drank. He got an indecipherable look as a reward, something between puzzlement and indignation.

"I've been thinking—"

"I was afraid of that."

Ben slapped Chris on the arm and laughed. "I've been thinking about having a son. What to do. How would you feel if I engaged the MPA to rescue my son and bring him to me?"

"I'd tell you you were fucking insane. We were lucky to get out of this alive and relatively unscathed. You don't want to take them on again, Ben. We might not do so well next time."

"We'd have nine months to plan it. And I've still got the dust. We could go back, get my child..." He swallowed. He didn't want to say this, but he knew he'd feel like a complete bastard if he didn't. "I've got a free pass to wherever it is the Gandharvas come from. So we can get Geoff back too. What do you think?"

Chris drew himself more closely together. His head lowered fractionally, and there was that score in his brow, like someone had hit him with a hammer between the eyes. "I'm sorry," he said. "Sorry I made a scene...am *still* making a scene. Just ignore me. I'll be fine in the morning."

"We could—"

The restraint snapped, let out a flood of words: "You can't rescue a man from something he's chosen. It was true, what he said. We never really looked past the end of the war—didn't expect to survive it, you see. It didn't matter then that everything would change, after. We were living from day to day, didn't think about the future. Probably we always would have drifted apart. He'd have wanted a wife, children. I'd have embarrassed him—it would have all ended badly. Probably just as well we've been spared that."

It had the flavour of something he'd been telling himself repeatedly since he got home, and it made Ben unhappy. He reached out and curved a hand around Chris's cheek, feeling beard burn and the soft fragility of human skin, warm and frail.

Chris covered the hand with his own. "I don't want you to think this means I care about you any less, Ben. It's just, the war was the biggest thing in our lives. Not the best, the way you're the best. But the most intense. It's hard...to get over it. You know?"

You're the best thing in my life? "Was that..." *A declaration of love?* Ben rather thought it might be, phrased in cripplingly undemonstrative 1940s speak. All at once, he didn't want to think about going up against the Sidhe again for a long time either. He'd think about that later. "Never mind. Listen, let's go to bed, yeah. You're tired, I'm tired. I don't remember the last time I slept, and you look like shit. Come on."

Chris's bed was as warm as he remembered, and as comforting. He tucked himself around Chris, who responded by fitting his head under Ben's chin and holding on tight. They were relaxing moment by moment, bodies slackening and the afternoon filling up with delightfully illicit slumber, when Chris murmured against his throat. "I thought you were going to stay."

"With *them*?" Oh, that explained a hell of a lot. Ben watched the tossed shadows of leaves swirl on the bedroom ceiling, shifted a little so that he could card his fingers through the soft hair and prickly stubble at the nape of Chris's neck. "That was never going to happen. I wanted to come home. Thought you knew that."

A sigh, weary but also relieved. "So glad. Don't know what I'd have done, really. Without you. Gone to pieces, probably."

Chris's breath was alternately warm and cold against the hollow of Ben's throat. "Drunk myself to an early grave."

Ben extended his petting, running his fingers through newly washed hair, and tried to think of a way of saying *I may have been out of it, but I know what you did for me*, that didn't convey any sense that he was here because of favours owed. Neither of them, he hoped, was the kind of bloke who felt that the princess owed her rescuer sex, or why would he do it?

"I was always going to come home to you. Thought you knew that. Idiot."

Chris laughed, a whisper of drowsy amusement, roused himself briefly to say, "So I'm not getting it wrong, this time? This is boyfriend stuff, am I right?"

"This is boyfriend stuff," Ben acknowledged, and for a moment found himself so transparent and fragile with joy he feared to move in case he shattered. "Go to sleep, okay? I think it's over. We got out, it's finished, and now we've got a future ahead of us. If I wasn't so tired, I'd kiss you."

"I'm all yours…" The words trailed off into silence. Ben's heavy eyelids closed, and sleep, delicious and dark, pulled itself over him like a quilt.

Chris woke, torn out of dreamless sleep to the sound of engines. They rattled the window, roared and throbbed through the profound quiet of early dawn. He was out of bed and stuffing himself into trousers before he remembered this couldn't be a dawn raid, couldn't be German Dorniers—no air-raid siren, no batman shaking him awake. But that was still the earthshaking throb of propeller engines he heard, making the water in its glass on his bedside tremble and Ben sit up, looking bleary and disgruntled, beautiful with his bed hair and the sleep in his onyx eyes.

"What the hell is it now?"

"I don't know," Chris said, though he had a hope burning beneath his breastbone like fairy gold. "Come on!"

They tumbled down the stairs and out into the back garden. Dawn was a pearl-coloured wash across the eastern sky, and then the first arm of the sun slid out from beneath the horizon, and the river in front of Chris's house turned to gold as the sky above lightened to silver and citrus. Behind them, the moon still hung white in a pale blue sky, and above a flight of geese arrowed, their wings blazing against the sky, their calls completely drowned out by the distinctive *whuum, whuum, whuum* of a Lancaster banking, the four mighty engines dopplering against each other in what sounded like the beat of a great heart.

They stood in the dawn freshness, feet in the dewy grass and watched as she came about—little more than a sketch in strokes of light against the lightening sky, transparent as though she were made of glass, though Chris knew perfectly well she was now as tough as diamond.

He looked up and waved madly at the smudges of men he could see through the smudges of Perspex. Too hard to see if they waved back, but she waggled her wings in salute as she came over again, turned, one more roaring pass, so close she almost clipped the chimney, and then she began to climb, straight for the rising sun.

He watched until she was swallowed up by the blaze, was incredibly grateful when Ben disappeared inside without a word, leaving him to get his emotions under control and school his face out of the contortion of joy and ridiculous tears. "Good luck, boys," he said at last, and standing up straight gave them a final salute.

Then he went indoors to find the kettle was on, and an early delivery of papers lay on the doormat. He handed them to Ben, who was sitting at the kitchen table with his feet stretched out before him, and started to cook breakfast. He felt suddenly a great need for bacon and eggs.

"It says here..." Ben looked up as Chris put a mug of coffee in front of him. The folded paper he held showed a blurry picture of outlandish people taken with a night vision camera. "...that a police helicopter was called in to break up an unauthorised fireworks display at a live role-playing convention yesterday night. Up by the Nine Ladies."

He turned a page, smoothed it out. The bacon sizzled in the pan and the scent of it permeated the kitchen. Chris examined his feelings again and discovered that beneath the quiet awe and joy of the sight of his crew going home, he was still a little bruised. But that should heal in time, and time was something he now had. "Is that so?"

"Oh, and apparently there was a midair collision between a stolen Mosquito and the Tornado sent to intercept it. Both pilots killed."

Chris kicked the door open, and the stray cat who always breakfasted here slid in and wound about Ben's ankles, purring. "He was a hero," he said, turning the bacon, cracking the eggs into the pan. "That pilot. No one will ever know."

Ben's quick smile deserved to inspire a sonnet, but Chris wasn't much of a hand with poetry.

"That makes two of you then."

"Just *don't*. All right?" Chris decanted the eggs and bacon onto plates. He brought them over and set them on the table with brown sauce and salt. The cat got her own slice, which she pulled straight off the saucer it was served on and played with like a mouse, spreading grease over the kitchen floor, much to Ben's disgust.

"It's all part of the job, isn't it? And this..." Chris dropped a kiss on the edge of that smile, saw it widen in response. All of this—keeping the home fires burning, honey still for tea, crows cawing in the garden outside, friends to phone and reassure, someone to come home to at night—this was what it was all about. "You and me. This was what it was all for."

A future, Ben had said, and yes, it was time he stopped living in the past and finally learned to be here, now, working towards a future.

"Speaking of which, are you still interested in a job with the MPA?"

Ben laughed and nudged him with his bare foot under the table. "Are you joking? You couldn't keep me away if you tried."

About the Author

Alex Beecroft was born in Northern Ireland during the Troubles and grew up in the wild countryside of the Peak District. She studied English and Philosophy before accepting employment with the Crown Court where she worked for a number of years. Now a stay-at-home mum and full-time author, Alex lives with her husband and two daughters in a little village near Cambridge and tries to avoid being mistaken for a tourist.

Alex is only intermittently present in the real world. She has led a Saxon shield wall into battle, toiled as a Georgian kitchen maid, and recently taken up an 800-year-old form of English folk dance, but she still hasn't learned to operate a mobile phone.

You can find me in many places, but chiefly at my website http://alexbeecroft.com.

The faeries at the bottom of the garden are coming back—with an army.

Bomber's Moon
© 2012 Alex Beecroft
Under the Hill, Part 1

When Ben Chaudhry is attacked in his own home by elves, they disappear as quickly as they came. He reaches for the phone book, but what kind of exterminator gets rid of the Fae? Maybe the Paranormal Defense Agency will ride to his rescue.

Sadly, they turn out to be another rare breed: a bunch of UFO hunters led by Chris Gatrell, who—while distractingly hot—was forcibly retired from the RAF on grounds of insanity.

Shot down in WWII—and shot forward seventy years in time, stranded far from his wartime sweetheart—Chris has been a victim of the elves himself. He fears they could destroy Ben's life as thoroughly as they destroyed his. Chris is more than willing to protect Ben with his body. He never bargained for his heart getting involved.

Just when they think there's a chance to build a life together, a ghostly voice from Chris's past warns that the danger is greater than they can imagine. And it may take more than a team of rank amateurs to keep Ben—and the world—out of the elf queen's snatching hands…

Warning: Brace yourself for mystery, suspense, sexual tension, elves in space and a nail-biting cliffhanger ending.

Available now in ebook and print from Samhain Publishing.

Enjoy the following excerpt from Bomber's Moon...

Ben studied the gesture of self-control. His mouth turned up at the ends. "Thinking bad thoughts, Wing Commander?"

Arrogant little sod. What did he expect Chris to say with Grace in the room? Oh, Ben might have poured out the whole story—the boy was young, and youngsters these days had no shame when it came to sex...

Wait, though, that was an interesting thought. Youngsters had no shame these days, and there Ben was, smiling like he'd got one over on Chris. It came up like the lava in a lamp, shouldering everything aside with a great glossy welling up of relief; Ben was smirking.

And smirking was not, perhaps, the expression of a victim, of a man betrayed. Not even of a man embarrassed and ill at ease. If anything, Ben was exuding the smugness of a man who'd found buried gold and intended to keep it all to himself.

"Bad thoughts, Mr. Chaudhry? I never have anything but the best of thoughts, and my instincts are splendid."

"For an old man."

Oh, Chris swallowed. That was...uncalled for. And rather delightful. "If you have complaints, I will of course try harder next time."

"Harder? How much harder?"

Grace set her flask down on the work surface with a click, leaned back, crossing her arms. They both started guiltily. Just for a moment it had been as though she hadn't been there at all. "I don't think I want to know what this is about." She pursed her lips, raised her eyebrows, then snorted, blowing out exasperation through her nose. "I can see I'm in the way. Here."

She handed the vial of water to Ben, who sniffed at it cautiously, the little plastic stopper held in his other hand. "It smells of snuff. I thought you said there wasn't any witchcraft in this."

Grace chuckled. "I think it's funny—holy water in an imp. The smell does cling, though, even when you've used all the perfume up and washed the bottle twice. Think of it as the odour of sanctity. I know I do."

"And this"—Ben looked askance at the tiny test tube full of water, with its plastic lid and remnant of torn-off label—"will protect me from…them…so well I can go back to work?"

"Yes." Grace poured out a cup of very stewed tea and gulped it down. "It needs to be on you at all times, though. I suggest you sew it into one of those tennis sweatbands that goes around your wrist—something you can sleep in. Don't take it off. If you've had the sort of fright that makes coming for help to Matlock Paranormal seem sensible, then you don't want to risk ever putting this down. Not until the larger problem is sorted. All right? And bear in mind that you haven't even addressed the larger problem yet. That has to be done if you're to be secure in the long run. This isn't a solution. This is just buying you time."

Ben looked at the door with an expression of uncertainty. Chris had not shut it properly and the wind, gusting over the peaks, kept opening and closing it—a stripe of bright morning and the skirl of cold, granite-scented air, and a creak and thud as it shut again. "What do I have to do to get rid of them permanently?"

"You could convert." Grace refolded her arms and the brief moment of cordiality was over.

"Even that might not help," Chris said. "Remember Tam Lin? The old star on his brow? But they still grabbed him and held him."

Responsibility hit Chris like flying into turbulence. There was nothing beneath his wings holding him up. He fell, heart in mouth, hands slippery on the joystick, brought the nose up, increased speed and won through, plunging back into confidence on the other side. They would not get Ben. He didn't know what to do to prevent it, but he *would*. Dying in the attempt was acceptable, but failing was not.

Wiping his hands on his shirt, he wished for a shower. Wished, in a moment of weakness, that he had left all of this alone, as the RAF had advised—or that all of it would have been content to leave *him* alone. But that way lay madness. You couldn't un-see what you'd seen, or un-know what you'd known. Besides, he'd never have met Ben if it wasn't for *them*.

SAMHAIN
PUBLISHING

It's all about the story...

Romance

HORROR

Retro ROMANCE

www.samhainpublishing.com

CPSIA information can be obtained at www.ICGtesting.com
Printed in the USA
BVOW07s1410080813

328185BV00004B/220/P